FALLEN ANGELS
By
W.H. BESWICK

COPYRIGHT2020@W.H.BESWICK

This story is a work of fiction and the product of the writer's imagination. Any resemblance to any person, place, institution, or event is coincidental.

AUTHOR'S NOTE: THERE IS NO MOUNTAIN CALLED KC-15 IN ALASKA OR ANYWHERE ELSE IN THE WORLD. AFTER AN EXTENSIVE SEARCH (THANK YOU, GOOGLE), THE AUTHOR COULD NOT FIND A MOUNTAIN TO FIT HIS DESIRED NEEDS, SO THE WRITER CREATED ONE. AS POINTED OUT, THIS IS A WORK OF FICTION.

AUTHOR'S SECOND NOTE: I DID SOME RESEARCH, ACTUALLY TALKED TO SOME ROCK CLIMBERS AND USED GOOGLE. THERE IS STILL A DEBATE BETWEEN PITONS AND THE DEVICES NICKNAMED "FRIENDS." MY CHARACTER, ROSCOE, IS AGAINST THE USE OF PITONS. THIS WAS DONE FOR MORE COMICAL REASONS. I HAVEN'T EVER CLIMBED MOUNTAINS OF THIS SIZE. SO I CANNOT TAKE A STAND IN THIS DEBATE.

AUTHOR'S THIRD NOTE: THE AUTHOR HAS DECIDED TO USE MILITARY RANKS EARTH ARMED FORCES. RATHER THAN MAKEUP NAMES, THE ALIEN'S RANK WILL SERVE AS THEIR NAME. IS THE AUTHOR BEING LAZY? PROBABLY.

CHAPTER 1

The name of the planet and its location are really of no importance. It's a planet quite similar to Earth in many good and bad ways. The inhabitants look human, except for their bright green hair, yellow eyes, and grayish skin. They are smaller in stature but broader in girth. Their fingers are long and delicate.

Five of these aliens are standing in a great hall with white stone walls and floor. The floor appears to be polished marble. Above the main floor is a wraparound walkway with a low wall. Sunlight comes through several windows. A dome-shaped skylight of colorful glass is mounted in the center of the ceiling. Dozens of tables have been set up for what looks like a feast. Gold plates and matching utensils. Fruit, odd-shaped and different colors, fills scattered bowls.

The five aliens appear to be high officials. They are wearing brightly colored robes and too many silver and gold chains hanging around their necks. More brooches and ribbons add to the extravagant outfits. They walk around the hall looking quite smug, their hands clasped in front of them.

"All is ready for our guests," one alien says, nodding toward the door. "Just one last thing to make it perfect."

The double doors at the end of the great hall open. Two groups of taller and more muscular aliens march in. They carry silver rifles, twisted barrels, and wooden stocks. Their uniforms are a dull green with black trim down the legs. One of the aliens, who has a simple gold star on the front of his uniform, steps forward. They all snap to attention.

"Excellent. Captain, I want you and your men on the balconies and behind the wall. Wait to fire until they are seated. I will signal you by offering a toast."

"With all due respect, I have fought with them. I am uncomfortable with this course of action," the Captain says.

"I don't care what you are comfortable with...the war is over. It is time to return to a more peaceful society. One I doubt you will fit into. Now..."

The dome skylight shatters as soldiers dressed in black uniforms and helmets come crashing through. Gold visors cover their faces. They drop down but then hover midair a few feet above the floor. Even more soldiers come crashing through the double doors. The invading soldiers open fire. Small black-and-gold mini-rifles blast out yellow beams. The captain and his men are cut down in seconds. They drop to the floor, looking more stunned than hurt. The officials find themselves surrounded by the invading soldiers.

"Don't shoot! Don't shoot!" the lead official cries, holding his hands in front of his chest.

One solider hovering drops to the floor as gracefully as a dancer. This soldier steps forward. There is a single silver braid around one shoulder of her uniform.

"Your life is in no danger...at the moment." The soldier pulls off the helmet, revealing a beautiful face with sharp features. Her skin is a very subtle green. Purple eyes that almost seem to shine take in the officials. A long, thick braid of silver hair hangs down the middle of her back. A smile comes to her lips. "I must apologize for our early arrival. It appears we have spoiled your little surprise. Although, I must tell you, I am not fond of surprises."

Still smiling, she touches a small silver-and-black bracer on her wrist as she enters the room and table. She glances down at the fallen troops. "Not to worry, your men are stunned by our sudden appearance. The room is secure, Commander."

Like the female, a male soldier casually walks into the hall. He is taller and has a thicker build. His hair is cut into a flat top, which suits his square face. There is a scar on one side of his face. It is not disfiguring. It adds character to his face. His uniform is also black, with two gold braids on each shoulder. He stops to pick up a bottle of wine and reads the label. "A local label. How disappointing. I would think saving your planet would at least merit a nice import. This really should be chilled."

The officials look down at their feet. Once again, the leader steps forward. "Commander, I don't understand; we're here to celebrate our victory."

"Our victory?" Commander says with puzzlement as he looks down at the soldiers on the floor. "An interesting choice of words. Don't you think so, Captain?"

"They did hire us, and we did win," Captain says with a sly grin. "Some sort of celebration would be expected."

"So we do have reason to celebrate?" Commander asks, walking right up to the official.

"We certainly do, Commander," the official answers tremblingly.

"It was nice of you to invite the royal guard to the celebration," he says, glancing back at the soldiers.

"To honor you..."

"Do I look like a fool to you?" Commander asks, and his casual tone doesn't change as he looks into the alien's face.

"No, Commander, you don't..."

"Then do not treat me like one. You hired us to free you from the Utars. You are now free. It is now time to pay us for this service. I lost too many friends on this job, so I am not in the mood for lies. Or betrayals."

"Commander, we were desperate when we contacted you. The Utars destroyed most of our cities. Those they didn't kill, they kept as slaves or sold to be used, sold into a life of slavery. Our vault is nearly empty. We have nothing."

Captain points her weapon at the official. Commander gives her a quick look, and she lowers it.

"Show me this empty vault." His voice is still soft, almost friendly.

"Certainly," the official says with a sigh of relief. "If you and your men will follow me to the treasury building."

"Not that vault," the Commander says with a small smile. It's the vault in the palace throne room that I am not supposed to know about."

The Officials all become nervous. Captain, smiling, wanders over but looks at Commander. The officials notice this and look to Commander. "Commander, I have no idea..."

"Show me, or I will have my Captain kill you." His voice is now cold as ice.

"Commander..."

Captain uses her weapon to destroy the wine bottles on the table. The blood-red liquid spreads over the white tablecloth and appears to smoke. Captain seems amused. "You were right, sir; it was a not very good vintage."

Commander, for the first time, shows some emotion: anger. He pulls his pistol and puts it under the official's chin. He snatches up an unbroken bottle, breaks the top, and holds the jagged bottle up in front of the alien's face. "Show me now, or I will make you drink every drop of this!"

CHAPTER 2

WE ARE SOLDIERS. NOT THEIVES.

A low humming fills a pitch-dark room. Light fills the room slowly as a large round metal door swings open. Lights click on, revealing stacks of metal boxes and other golden artifacts, including several crowns, scepters, and orbs. There are even two jewel-encrusted thrones.

Commander, Captain, and several soldiers come into the room. The official is pulled along and pushed against the wall.

Commander goes to a box and pulls it open. It is filled with colorful gems that flicker in the dim light. He scoops up a handful of the stones and lets them filter through his fingers. "Now, what do we have here? Star gems. Since coming to your world, I have longed to see them."

Captain picks up one gem and holds the glowing jewel in her hand. "This is one of the most beautiful things I have seen in a long time."

"You hear that, bureaucrat?" Commander says, looking at the angry man. "You could learn a thing or two from my Captain."

The alien just shrugs, even finding the courage to glare at Commander. Commander closes the lid and steps back. He looks at the official and shakes his head. "You don't understand. Maybe you never will. War makes you appreciate the simpler things in life. Thank you for your generosity. I and my men can return home with something to show for our absence and ease the pain of the families who lost loved ones here."

Commander nods at the Captain, who turns to her troops.

"All right, let's get these boxes out of here," Captain snaps.

The soldiers quickly grab the boxes and carry them out.

"Commander, you can't take it all!" the official cries, stepping forward. "We'll starve. How will we rebuild our world?"

"You are sitting ON some of the richest mines in this part of the galaxy," Commander says with an amused tone. "I have my doubts. You will not starve. We are not taking everything, just what is owed us."

"The mines have to be worked," the official says, moving forward. Things have changed. "The ones who fought alongside you, like you, expect payment for your services. They demand to be paid for their work."

"Before we came, they lived in fear of you. Why does it surprise you that your people were slaves who fought with us? While you safely hid, this world is now more theirs than yours. I suggest you grab a shovel, start digging, or share the wealth." Commander pushes the official aside. Captain walks over to a table covered with jewel-encrusted crowns and scepters.

"I suppose it would be in bad taste to steal the crown jewels?" she asks, fingering a crown.

"Captain, we have spent the last year fighting in the mud and rain to free these people from an invader who raped and plundered their world." Commander comes over to the crowns and picks up a jeweled orb. "So I ask you, are we soldiers or thieves?"

"We are soldiers."

"Leave them, and we will take what is rightfully ours."

"Yes, sir."

Captain and Commander follow their men out. The Official looks around the vault, which is empty except for the royal jewels.

CHAPTER 3

IT'S NEVER EASY

Another soldier, dressed in a black uniform with a red braid on his shoulder, speaks into his arm bracer. "I'm at the hangar. Where are you?"

The sound of running feet makes him look up. The soldier smiles almost as the Commander and Captain rush up. Their soldiers carrying the boxes from the vault are right behind them. The commander stops in front of the Colonel. He is a young man but with the same features. "Did the fleet get off?"

"Yes, sir," Colonel says. "We are the last ship."

"Have the Techs run a status check on the ship and prepare for lift-off," Commander snapped, watching his men carry the boxes onboard.

"Commander, we have a problem," Colonel says, pointing to ten dead bodies. "Two of our own betrayed us. They got to the techs, but I got to them."

"Greed has become our greatest enemy," Commander says. "Did you check out the ship?"

"Of course. Everything seems to be functioning, but I'm not a tech."

A soldier runs up to Captain and whispers something in her ear. She nods and turns. "Commander, our men, and the jewels are all loaded. We can lift off when ready."

"We can't lift off," Colonel says worriedly. "All our techs are dead."

Commander looks at the ship and closes his eyes. He thinks for a moment. "We can't stay here. Our former employers will come looking. This time with more than the Royal Guard."

"If our ship breaks down, who will repair it?"

"We can assume the fleet has already made the jump, so they will be no help," Commander says.

"We have the computer. It should be of help if something breaks down," Captain says. "Once we make the jump, we send a distress call to the fleet. They may still be in range. Anything is better than staying here."

Commander paces around the hangar. Sighing, he looks at his officers. "Captain is right. We can't stay here. Get the men aboard."

"Commander..." Colonel says, still not sure.

"Colonel! Move!"

"Commander, I must protest."

"Colonel, stop your whining. Prepare the ship for takeoff. Move!"

Colonel just nods and walks off. Commander watches the man and slams his fist against the ship's side.

CHAPTER 4

WE HAVE A FALLEN ANGEL

A small radar station sits in the middle of a snow-covered wasteland. It is nothing more than a small, two-story metal and brick building with a giant metal dish beside it. The howling wind and snow whipping around make the station seem even more isolated.

Four men wearing blue jumpsuits with United States Air Force patches are huddled around three radar screens. The small room is filled with electronic gear, including a computer from another age. All four men stare at the screens. A green blip moves across them.

"So, what do we do?" one of the men asks.

"So we all agree this is not a weather balloon or one of ours," another says. "Look at the size of that thing."

"Looks like someone else saw," a third man says when two more blips appear on the screen. "Here come our interceptors."

"That thing is really moving," the first says, then gasps. "Oh my God! Our guys are gone."

"What is this thing?" someone asks.

"Whatever it is, it's going down," the first man says. "It's slowing. It's not crashing... its landing."

He grabs a phone and dials. Without waiting for a response, he says, "We have a fallen angel. Two of our planes are down."

CHAPTER 5

DEACON

The man, known simply as Deacon, sits in an office without windows. Shelves filled with books line three of the walls. The metal door does not fit with the bookshelves, red carpet, or large oak desk. A computer sits on a side table by the desk, and paper files neatly stacked surround the man. A red landline push-button phone sits on the corner of the desk.

Deacon is a large African-American man with a bald head. The tailor-made pinstriped suit suggests a muscular body. A red carnation sits on the lapel of his jacket. Gold, wire-rimmed glass rests on his nose. He sits quietly at his desk, his eyes closed, his hands tented in front of him. It's almost like he is meditating.

The red phone rings. Deacon's eyes open. He casually picks up the phone. "I've been waiting for your call. Has it been confirmed? Two planes down. Is the military securing the area? Yes, sir. I'm assembling a team as a backup right away. Yes, sir, we may get this one fully intact, along with its inhabitants. No, sir; if it falls to us, we will not drop the ball."

CHAPTER 6

It is a massive room with no windows. It has been built for functionality and ascetics. Tables fill the room, cluttered with tools and electronic bits and pieces. One table has three computers on it. In the center of the room is a laser weapon. It sits on a round base. The backend is a long silver cylinder. What looks like glass tubes stick out of the cylinder? A small console is mounted to the side of the weapon.

An air vent pops off the wall. Brett Taylor's head comes out. He looks around, smiles, and climbs out. He is in his mid-thirties and has a slender but muscular build. His blonde hair is cut short. He would be considered handsome, except for his eyes. They are blue and show nothing. He is dressed in black, with a knapsack strapped to his back.

Watershaw, a young man with black hair, is dressed just like Brett. Unlike Brett, he looks nervous.

"Okay, we're in," Brett says, looking very pleased. His smile has no warmth in it.

"Yeah, but we got about five minutes before their security arrives," Watershaw says, looking around.

"More than enough time. Let's move."

Brett trots over to one of the computers and begins to type. The screen clicks on and fills with data. He inserts a USB drive and waits. "I'll get the data. You get the photos."

Watershaw, still nervous, pulls out a small camera and begins to take pictures of the weapon. He looks over and asks, "How do we get out of here?"

"I got it covered," Brett snaps, moving to the second computer. "Just do your job."

Watershaw glares at him but keeps taking pictures. Brett moves onto the last computer. He types, puts in another USB, moves back to the first computer, and pulls out the USB. Brett pulls off his pack and pulls out a wad of plastic explosives with a timer. He puts this on the tower. The spy moves down the computers, taking the sticks and placing bombs. He turns to Watershaw. "Done."

"One last shot," Watershaw says. He takes the picture and looks over at Brett. "What's with the bombs? Deacon's orders were to get the data and leave."

"Watershaw, you got to learn to read between the lines," Brett says. He puts a giant bomb on the laser and sets the timer. Then he takes Watershaw's camera and pockets it.

Brett pulls Watershaw over to the door and pushes him against the wall. He pulls out his pistol and cocks it. Watershaw nervously follows his lead. The doors swing open; four security guards rush in with their pistols.

"Right on cue," Brett says with a smile. He shoots two of the guards with two bullets. It takes Watershaw four shots to take out one guard. The last guard drops to the floor, rolls over, and fires. Watershaw is hit and goes down. Brett shoots the man with casual indifference. One of the computers explodes into a small fireball. Brett dives out of the room as the last computer explodes. The bomb on the laser goes off, engulfing the entire room.

Brett is thrown down the hall and against the wall. He shakes his head and stands up. He seems to be stunned. An elevator dings. This brings him out of it. He looks over as three guards emerge from the elevator. He empties his pistol. One of the men goes down. Brett kicks a door open and rolls out as the remaining guards fire their pistols.

Brett manages to get to his feet. He is in a stairwell and runs down the stairs, reloading his pistol. He stops to put a bomb on one of the steps. The sound of the guards makes him take off. He fires up at them before ducking through another door.

The two guards follow him down the stairs, yelling into their radios. The bomb goes off. The entire stairwell is engulfed in fire and smoke.

The blast sends Brett to the floor in a room filled with office cubicles. The door flies over his head and smashes into some cubicles. Brett staggers up and runs across the office area. The sprinklers click on, drenching Brett and everything else.

Brett runs up to the elevator just as the door opens. A young man in a suit just stands there. Brett grabs the man by his tie and pulls him out. He shoves the man to the floor and jumps into the elevator.

Brett takes out another bomb and sets it. He checks his pistol and takes a couple of deep breaths.

Four guards are on duty in the lobby. One is on the phone, calling the fire department. Two are sitting at the console, watching the computer screens. The last one is by the glass door; it looks like he is waiting for someone.

The elevator doors open. Brett tosses out the bomb and closes the door. The bomb goes off. Another fireball engulfs the lobby. All four guards are killed, and the glass doors and windows are shattered by the blast.

The elevator doors open. Brett runs out of the building and jumps into a brand-new black Mustang. He drives off just as two security cars come around the corner. They pull to a stop in front of the building as Brett vanishes around another corner. He laughs as he drives but becomes annoyed when his phone beeps. He pulls it out and looks at the face. "Mission completed."

"New assignment. Report to Alaska," a voice says.

"What the hell is in Alaska besides snow and bears?"

"Where is Roscoe?"

"Colorado, but he won't come," Brett says with a smile. "He ended up in the hospital last time."

"Convince him. He is really needed."

"I will try. Can you tell me who else is on the team and what this is about?"

"We need Roscoe to get you up KC-15."

"That's a mountain, I assume?" Brett asks, but no one answers. The phone beeps. The caller hung up. He nervously stares at the phone. This is the first time they just hung up on him. Did they already know he exceeded his orders? They would definitely be pissed about Watershaw. Brett has always worked alone until this mission. He's now worried that the young agent was there...to do what? Babysit him? Report him? He nervously chews on the end of his thumb. Okay, he crossed the line. Again. He could fix this. The first thing to do is to get Roscoe up to Alaska. That might take some doing. Brett pulls over to the curb and just stays there. He needs to think. Think. Think. Think.

CHAPTER 7

THE SOLDIER

A black helicopter flies over the Amazon jungle. The only light comes from the helicopter and the moon. Walter, dressed in green camo, leans out the side door. He can't be more than twenty. The young soldier is trying hard to look tough and hide his fear. "There is the clearing."

The chopper hovers over the clearing. Suddenly, the quiet is broken by gunfire and explosions. A few seconds later, a large man runs out of the clearing. Tommy Samson is a full-blooded Apache. He is a giant man with muscles that didn't come from a gym. His black hair is shaggy, falling over his ears. Dark eyes, sharp nose, and chiseled cheekbones give him a distinctive face. He is dressed in green camo, but it's filthy with mud and what may be blood. Samson carries an SA80 in his hands. He doesn't fire. He is running for his life toward the chopper.

The black chopper swoops in and hovers a few inches off the ground. Samson runs across the clearing, shedding unwanted gear. The clearing turns into a war zone as explosions hit the clearing. Gunfire fills the air.

Samson is knocked down a few times but manages to get up. He barely reaches the chopper in one piece. Walter points his Uzi at Samson and snaps, "Password!"

Samson looks up at Walter in shock. "Are you crazy?"

"Orders! How do I know you are Samson?"

Bullets begin to hit the chopper. The pilot looks back and yells, "Any day now!"

Samson moves like a machine as he slams his fist into Walter's gut, knocks the Uzi out of his hands, and shoves him back into the chopper. He climbs in and puts his boot on Walter's chest. "Another day, I would have killed you."

The chopper lifts off and flies over the jungle.

Samson slumps back in one of the seats. The kid gets up from the floor, glaring at him. He's about to say something but changes his mind. Right now, Samson is the alpha in this chopper. His dark eyes close. God, his legs are on fire. His back hurts, too. A few years ago, he would have just tossed the kid out of the chopper and told the pilot to go. Was he getting soft? Maybe he is getting too old for this kind of crap. That would explain the legs and the pounding in his chest. This was supposed to be his last mission. He hadn't completed it because he had been called back. They needed him somewhere else. He reminded them this was supposed to be his last. They pointed out he still needed to complete it. He still owed them one. They tried to soften the blow by telling him the fee was higher.

How much longer can he do this? He needs to count the number of places he's been. Places that no one in their right mind would go to. Jungles, deserts, and war-torn cities are now all blurring into one big mess. A mess that was inside his head. Samson had money, just no time to spend it. He opens his eyes and looks at the kid. "Do you know where I am going?"

"Like they would tell me?" he growls.

Samson just smiles and says, "Sorry about the punch. It's been a long day."

"For both of us," Henry says, finally smiling. "Where it is, I think it is cold. But you didn't hear that for me."

"Who am I going to tell?" Samson says and closes his eyes.

CHAPTER 8

THE SCIENTIST

Yoshiko Sasaki is in her thirties, an attractive woman with long hair pinned into a messy bun. Goggles cover her brown eyes. Her lips are squeezed into a thin line as she studies a silver tube with gold, curly wires sticking out at odd angles. "Where do you go?"

The scientist is standing in a long, expansive room with a grid painted on the floor. Each square contains a piece of metal, electronics, or machine parts. There are no windows; the only way in is a large steel door. Two men in black uniforms stand at rigid attention, arms behind their backs, guarding the door.

Off to one side are three technicians working what looks like the charred, twisted remains of some kind of device. It's mostly melted into a black block, but there is still evidence that it did something. They mainly study it, occasionally poking with gloved fingers. One furiously takes notes on his iPad.

Stan, a young man in a lab coat, comes up behind Yoshiko and waits. She doesn't seem to notice him or just doesn't care that he is there.

"Figure it out yet?"

Still ignoring him, Yoshiko takes off her goggles and walks over to the large piece of jagged metal with some small electronic attached to it, leaning against a wall. Yoshiko holds up the piece in front of the metal. Stan follows her and watches.

"This goes right about here, or maybe over here," Yoshiko says, more to herself than Stan. She pulls out a dog-eared journal and makes some notes.

"Do you really think you can rebuild this thing?" Stan asks.

"Oh, Stan. Glad you're here. I was thinking..." Yoshiko says in a distracted tone but stops to look at what could be an engine part on the floor. She retrieves it and holds it up. Stan moves it around, studying it from different angles.

"You were thinking..." Stan asks.

"Oh yes." She is still distracted as she studies the part. "I was thinking we should go back to the crash site. I think we might have missed a few parts."

"I'd say a lot more than a few. Admit it, Yoshiko. This is all guesswork."

"Stan, most of science is guesswork. Except we call it a hypothesis."

"It would help if we knew what this was. Is it a prototype we made, or is this the real deal?"

Yoshiko ignores his question and goes to what looks like a futuristic control panel. "I'm going to take this apart. We are missing something."

"Yoshiko, you were supposed to be in class five minutes ago."

Yoshiko looks at her watch. "Damn! Why did I have to teach classes?"

"So they can pay you more money."

Yoshiko rushes over to a desk, tosses her journal into a briefcase, and closes it. She grabs her suitcase and a couple of large books. The scientist walks to the door. The guards don't move. Looking annoyed, she fumbles in her jacket and pulls out her ID. They step aside and open the door. "You know, I can understand wanting my ID coming in but when I leave? Really? A little much."

Neither of the men says a word.

Yoshiko goes out the door. It leads to a stairwell that goes up several flights, but no other doors exist. The scientist glares at the stairs, sighs, and starts to climb. She is a little winded by the time she reaches another metal landing. She has to swipe her ID, punch in a code, and then put her eye before a scanner.

"You have three seconds to exit the site," a robotic voice says. "Three. Two."

"Yeah, yeah," Yoshiko says, pushing open the door and going out.

"Have a nice day," the robot voice says.

The scientist steps out onto what looks like an Ivy League college campus: old buildings covered with ivy, green lawns, trees, and students rushing around. The scientist struggles with her stuff but stops when a black sedan pulls up right in front of her. Some students notice the car blocks her path because she is walking on the grass. Two men dressed in black suits with sunglasses climb out. One holds up his ID. "Dr. Sasaki, a moment of your time."

Yoshiko barely glances at the ID. "You guys really blend in. I would have never guessed you were government spooks. The university is going to be pissed about you driving right onto the quad."

"We have a fallen angel."

"I already have one in my lab. At least, I think I do? Should go back. The class will survive without me." She says it to herself but then looks at the men. "I thought Dr. Lewis had dibs on the next one."

"Actually, it has been confirmed that it is a prototype you are working on. It didn't come from outer space. Aside from that, you are more qualified than Dr. Lewis."

"He might beg to differ."

"You are an expert mountain climber. Lewis isn't. So it's your lucky day."

"I only climb a couple times a year," Yoshiko says, looking annoyed. "You mean I have been wasting my time on...wait, it's on top of a mountain? What mountain?"

"Doctor, we are in a little bit of a rush. We're at a code seven."

"I hate this spy lingo. Is code seven good or bad?

Without a word, the agents practically shove her into the car.

"Wait..."

Yoshiko sits in the back of the car, glaring at the backs of the heads of the two men. There was no attempt to make small talk. Where did they get these guys? She hated this spy crap. All she wanted was to continue her research. Now, everything she had been learning came from good old Earth. "So this real, or another waste of my time?"

Nothing.

"I have a Nobel prize," she says, leaning forward. "So, it means I am pretty smart. I can keep a secret, or I wouldn't be in this car. Anything? Nothing."

The young scientist slumps back and looks around the interior of the car. "You know, my PhD thesis was titled. You guys would like it. Theories on the practicality of deep space travel. It was brilliant. Even got published. Don't suppose you guys read it? No."

Yoshiko closes her eyes and debates whether she has chosen the right career. She blames her father. He was really into UFO stuff. She not only grew up with it but got sucked in. Her whole education had been to...to what. To confirm what her father had taught her. There is life out there, and they have visited this planet. So when they came calling, she was all in. Maybe this one would be the one.

"Doctor, where is your climbing gear?" one of the men asks.

"At home in my attic."

"We will swing by there and pick up your gear. You may wish to change. You're going someplace very cold."

"Good to know. I was thinking of just wearing my bikini."

Nothing.

CHAPTER 9

Somewhere in the Colorado Nation Park sits a small building that serves as a ranger station and museum. It is made of logs with a wood shingle roof. The front porch sags, confirming it has seen better days. It sits in a small clearing surrounded by tall trees. A small dirt patch serves as a parking lot. A beat-up Jeep, an older Ford, and a brand-new Lexus are parked close to the open door.

The inside looks just as old and rundown. The room has a wooden counter and a cash register from another century. Behind the counter is a plastic display rack with maps, shirts, caps, and other souvenirs. The other side of the room is filled with glass cases. The display cases contain various flowers, pine cones, stuffed squirrels and chipmunks, and vintage photographs. The whole place looks very dusty, including the things on display.

Roscoe is in his late twenties or early thirties. It is tough to tell. He is short and slender, but his bare arms show more than a bit of muscle. His blond hair is a short mess of curls that don't reach his ears. There is a day-old beard on his square jaw. His blue eyes are wide and bright. His lips are curled into a smile that makes you think he is about to make a joke or say something clever. He is wearing old jeans and a tan ranger's uniform shirt. Both have seen better days. Roscoe stands before an old lady, a young boy, and a beautiful red-haired woman. Her stylish blouse and pants scream that she doesn't belong in the woods. The spike heels are not for hiking.

"As you can see, this pine cone is found all over the country," Roscoe says in a bored tone, pointing to a pine cone in a display case. The boy yawns. Roscoe continues his very dull lecture. "Now the Ponderosa pine cone..."

The old lady yawns. The redhead yawns and then smiles at him.

"It's just as boring as the last two. Thanks for coming," Roscoe says with a big smile. All donations to save your national parks are gladly accepted."

The old lady thanks him and walks out with the boy. The redhead stays and smiles at Roscoe. "This wasn't worth a dollar."

"You want a refund?" Roscoe says, moving closer.

"You're Roscoe. Is it true you've climbed every mountain in the world?"

"Not true. I have only climbed those mountains worth climbing."

"Why did you stop climbing? Was it because you fell?"

"You sound like a reporter but certainly don't look like one with those clothes. Rodeo Drive?"

"Some of it. You didn't answer the question."

"Repeating myself. I climbed every mountain worth climbing. At least, I thought I had." Roscoe smiles at her.

She shakes her head and smiles back. "Are you trying to be clever?"

"In my defense, I am out of practice. Middle of nowhere. Minimal occasion to work on my flirting techniques."

"That's not what Barbara said."

"Barbara. Oh yes, how is she?"

"Very married. You're very short for a legend."

"And you are very tall for whatever it is you do. Barbara worked for a climbing magazine. She was a fan. She found me charming. So, who are you?"

"You have a certain charm about you," the redhead concedes. "But still short."

"Does that mean no dinner?" Roscoe asks, looking crestfallen.

"I have to get home. Things to do."

"You didn't drive up here to look at stuffed squirrels and pine cones. You are not dressed for hiking or camping. Need help figuring out what you are and why you are here. By the way, I love that scent you are wearing. Now, about dinner."

"I love nature. Clean air."

"I can see why clean air is important to you." He smiles right into her face.

"Could you be any less subtle?"

"I told you I lost the knack. So, no dinner?"

"No dinner."

It is night when Roscoe rolls out of bed and stretches. He glances at the bed while pulling on his boxers. The redhead is curled up on the other side of the bed. Roscoe walks out, across his front room, and into the kitchen. He removes a beer from the fridge, opens it, and takes a swig. Roscoe goes back to the bedroom door and watches his companion sleep. He takes another pull on the beer, quietly thinking.

The redhead, Charlotte, worked for a production company. They wanted to hire him, but his shortness was a problem. Charlotte, who was called Charley by her close friends, had been discussing working around his shortness. One thing led to another.

Roscoe could use the money. Mountain climbing didn't pay that well. As a matter of fact, you had to hustle to get the money to start an expedition. He had a few endorsements but didn't play basketball or football. So the money was small.

She asked the same questions everyone had been asking since his last climb: *why did you retire? Was it because you fell?* Roscoe had dropped before. A lot.

Always walked away.

Roscoe had been thinking about that climb lately. A lot. He made no mistakes. It wasn't a particularly hard climb. He'd done it at least a dozen times. Why did he fall? It took a while to figure out what happened. He had lost focus. You can't lose focus. Especially when you are hanging on the side of a mountain. Finally, he had figured it out. He was bored. He conquered every mountain that was worth climbing. What was left for him? What does a retired mountain climber retire do?

Charley rolled over and muttered something.

Go to Hollywood? He had never really lived in a big city. He doubts he would like it. Roscoe drains his beer and goes back to the fridge for another. He drains that one when he's back at the bedroom door. "Well, Charley, I really don't have anything here."

He absentmindedly crushes the can.

"Go easy on that stuff; you're climbing tomorrow."

CHAPTER 10

JOB OFFER

Roscoe turns around and hits the light switch. Brett is sitting on the counter, sipping a Coke.

"Not with you. Please leave." His tone is cold.

"Your country needs you," Brett smiles and sips his coke.

"No," Roscoe snaps, goes to the fridge, gets another beer, and drains it defiantly. "See? In no condition to climb."

"You haven't heard what the job is."

"I have a good job."

"That's a lie. You only got two hundred in the bank."

"I get paid on Friday, so I'm good. Besides, I have discovered being a legend has certain benefits."

Brett slides off the counter and sneaks a peek at the redhead. "Now those are mountains worth climbing."

"God, you are so crude. No wonder you can't get any dates." Roscoe walks to his fridge and takes out another beer. He wiggles it at Brett, pops it, and takes a long drink. "Yup, that is the stuff."

"We're not here to discuss my social life."

Roscoe pushes Brett toward the front door with his beer in one hand. "Or lack of it. I am not going with you."

"Why not?" Brett asks, putting out his hands. "It will be fun!"

"Every time I go climbing with you, I get shot at. The last time I was hit."

"A scratch."

"I spent four weeks in the hospital. You want to see the scar?"

"I need the best. That would be you, good buddy."

"I am not your *good buddy*. Besides, the attractive lady in my bed has made me a better offer. I don't even have to climb a real mountain." He looks back into the bedroom. "Out of curiosity, what mountain are you planning to climb?"

"KC-15 in Alaska."

Roscoe begins to laugh and playfully hits Brett. Brett takes another drink from his coke. Roscoe keeps laughing as he takes another sip of his beer. "You are such a joker. You have to be kidding. Right? You're joking?"

"Difficult climb?" Brett asks, now looking serious.

"It has only been done once at this time of the year. By yours truly and three other very skilled climbers. We all almost fell. Several times. Going back down was discussed more than once. Once on top, we vowed never to do that again. Brett, as a professional mountain climber and someone who has climbed with you, you don't have the skill to climb that mountain."

"Then I really need you."

"Read my lips. *No.* There is nothing up there except snow, ice, rocks, and wind."

"Come on, Roscoe, it'll be a climb to brag about."

"Oh, bull. We both know I can't tell anyone about it if I go with you. Besides, I already got a great rep. Legend. Remember? Once again. What's up there that is worth risking your life for?"

"An experimental aircraft crashed with a full crew. It's a rescue mission."

Roscoe looks at Brett as he sips his beer and puts it down. "A chopper can get you up there a lot faster and with no danger of falling. You are not telling me so much. As a matter of fact, I am pretty sure you are lying."

"Already on the way, but there's a storm moving in. You're our backup plan."

"No way can we climb it in a storm. Haven't you watched any of those documentaries about mountain climbing? Those movies about Everest? You don't climb during a storm."

"This is not Everest."

"No, it is KC-15. Everest is a relatively easy climb. A blind guy did it. A guy with artificial legs did it. Everest is a test of your endurance. Most people don't make it to the top. Puking your guts out, risk of death to stand on top of the world for five minutes tops. It's stupid. Brett, it doesn't matter what the mountain is. You don't climb during a storm. Definitely not KC-15."

"Roscoe, it's really important," Brett says. Okay, you come with me to Alaska. Then you make the call on whether we climb or not."

"No shooting."

"No guns, I promise."

"Triple my usual fee. Whether we climb or not." Roscoe glances at the bed and thinks. "Pick me up in the morning."

"Our plane leaves in an hour."

"I need until morning to get my gear together."

"We both know you only need a half hour."

"Brett, you're not listening. This is a difficult climb. I need time to get my get my gear together."

Brett goes to the door and looks at the redhead. She rolls over and feels around for her lover. "Hey babe, can you get me something to drink? A beer would be great."

Roscoe takes another beer out of the fridge and smiles at Brett. "If you will excuse me, duty calls."

"You win. You may be in a better mood. I'm parked out back. Any chance I can sleep on the couch?"

"You have been working on that sense of humor," Roscoe says.

Brett finishes his Coke and quickly leaves. "Roscoe, you probably won't live to regret this."

CHAPTER 11

JUST HERE TO OBSERVE

KC-15 looks like it belongs in any other place other than Alaska. At first glance, you would think Disneyland Matterhorn is on steroids. It is a lot bigger and gives off an air of menace with its high peaks and the clouds swirling around it. All the rocks look black and jagged. The pointed snow caps make it look even more deadly. The base seems just as unwelcoming with the deep snow and dark pine trees. There is a large, flat-faced rock by the foot of the mountain. There are ten tin plates with names and dates on them. The words IN REMEMBERENCE OF are spray painted on it.

A makeshift camp has been set up at the base of the mountain. There are quite a few green army tents and soldiers. Many are rushing around, trying to prepare the remainder of the camp. Bright lights on poles are being erected around the camp. More men stand around, trying to stay warm, huddling over barrels with burning wood inside.

In the middle of this camp is a much larger tent. This one seems more stable than the small ones. Two armed soldiers are by the flap, guarding it while shuffling their feet in a feeble attempt to stay warm.

There are tables, chairs, and a cot set up in the tent. More importantly, two space heaters. General Parker is in his sixties but looks in excellent shape. His face is round, but not in a *chubby* way. He fills out the green fatigues very well. The only sign of his rank is the three stars on his shoulders. He twirls a very long cigar in his fingers.

Colonel Ryan is a younger man, but not by much. His face is like stone, but his grey eyes suggest he has seen some stuff. He is slender and wiry. There is nothing on his fatigues to indicate his rank.

Two much younger officers stand around the table, studying diagrams and photos. They glance over at the two men standing in front of the mountain diagram pinned to the side of the tent.

"Our satellites have spotted it right here," Parker says, using his cigar to point at a spot at the top of the mountain. Ryan takes notes as he studies the diagram.

"Could it be a new type of fighter or stealth?" Ryan asks. You know how tight-lipped those Air Force guys are."

"A saucer-shaped fighter. Wake up, Ryan. We all know what it is."

Deacon, wearing a long winter jacket with a fur collar and knit cap on his bald head, slips into the back of the tent but doesn't say a word. He just watches.

"We're both new to this situation," Parker says. "We'll handle it like a normal crash of an unknown craft. You know the drill. We send in the Thirty-Third to evaluate the situation."

"We prefer you not damage the craft," Deacon says softly, removing his gloves.

Ryan and Parker quickly turn toward Deacon. Deacon nods and pulls off his cap, then begins undoing his jacket. "It's warm in here."

Parker pulls out a lighter and fires up his cigar. "Deacon, you're not supposed to show up until I have the area secured."

"I feel perfectly safe in your hands," he says, wandering over to the table. He looks at the pictures but doesn't touch them. "The loss of two planes has changed the usual protocol, General Parker. Please go ahead with your briefing."

"I don't like it when you and your little C.I.A buddies show up ahead of schedule," Parker snaps.

"General?" Deacon says, looking up with genuine surprise. "Whatever makes you think I am with the C.I.A.? Sneaky little people with their bags of dirty tricks. Thank God I'm not C.I.A. Now, about the ship..."

"You're not C.I.A.?" Ryan asks, looking confused.

"Pardon my French, but who the hell are you with?" Parker sticks a cigar into his mouth.

"We're just a little agency whose only concern is our nation's security," he says, spreading his hands.

"Our national security is in danger?" Parker asks.

Deacon glances at the pictures and smiles. "Twenty-six hours ago, an unknown craft entered our air space, shot down two of our planes, and then planted itself on top of a mountain. You will note I used the word plant. Whatever is up there? Landed. I would consider that a threat."

"That makes it my job."

Deacon approaches the diagram and studies it. "Please don't concern yourself with me. I am simply an observer with the utmost confidence in your abilities to handle the present crisis."

Deacon goes over to another table and pours himself some coffee. The man seems utterly disinterested in the briefing. Parker and Ryan turn back to the chart. Parker once again uses his cigar as a pointer. "As I said, you and your men lift off in an hour. You will locate the craft and evaluate the situation."

"What are my options?" Ryan asks. "They've already shown themselves to be hostile."

"Take whatever actions you deem necessary. It would be preferable to take the craft in one piece and its occupants alive." Parker turns to Deacon. "I assume that is acceptable to you?"

Once again, Deacon smiles and sips his coffee. "General, this is your operation. Do as you please. My people would be thrilled if you could take the ship in one piece. Of course, if you should fail, I will be forced, with a heavy heart, to take over and reluctantly send in my own people."

Parker walks up to Deacon and growls. "I bet your people are already here."

"General, if my people were here, I would be predicting your failure. I would never do such a thing."

CHAPTER 12

ALL THIS FOR A PLANE CRASH

Roscoe sits by the window, watching the darkness and occasional cloud. The storm isn't here yet, but its coming. He can feel it in his bones. For a man who enjoys climbing the highest mountains in the world, it is interesting that he's always nervous when he flies. He had thought about it. It might be because he doesn't understand how a plane actually works. How does a thing so heavy get into the air? To him, it makes no sense. Of course, his degree is in forestry. He muses that it might be due to a lack of control. He has a certain degree of power even on the most dangerous mountain. Like he could decide to climb back down to the ground. Here, he is under the control of the pilot. Roscoe had met some pilots. This doesn't reassure him. Several were real jerks, and one in particular had a drinking problem.

Yet here he is. On a helicopter, that makes no sense to him, whatever. Their lives depend on a couple of blades spinning really fast.

Roscoe turns his attention to the other passengers. The man sitting across from him is enormous. His muscles developed for a reason. He looks Native American, but Roscoe isn't sure. *How do you ask that question in today's PC world?* You can't just ask. *So, what tribe are you with?* One thing is for sure, this guy is a soldier - but there are no patches on his fatigues. Is he one of those Special Forces guys?

Why did they need a Special Forces guy?

This is supposedly a rescue mission.

His eye drifts over to the woman. She's cute but has a crinkle in her brow. The whole flight, she had her nose stuck inside a journal that's seen better days. She occasionally glances out her window. Once, she looked over at Roscoe and smiled, then returned to her little journal.

Then there's Brett, once again slumped in his chair, looking bored. Roscoe thinks of the last time he went on one of Brett's missions. He got shot. Roscoe was not a spy, but he was convinced he got shot because of Brett. He would make a terrible mountain climber. The guy takes too many chances. Worse, he isn't careful. They are about to climb KC-15. He wasn't sure he could trust his old buddy. He definitely needs to gain the skill set to make this climb.

Roscoe looks at the other two. Neither one seems nervous. They may be good climbers or have yet to learn how difficult the climb will be. His glance passes the window. A blurry light comes into view. It grows sharper as the helicopter gets closer and begins its descent. A giant makeshift camp comes into view with lots of soldiers and equipment.

"My, my, all this for one crashed plane."

Samson opens his eyes. He had been trying to catch a few Z's before the climb. They drift over Roscoe, then out the window. He studies the camp below. "It does seem a bit much."

"What?" Yoshiko gasps, looking up from her journal. "You dragged my ass up here for a plane?"

All three looked at Brett, who didn't seem fazed by the curious stares. He put on what he considered his famous smile: "Don't ask me. I just work here."

"I get the feeling we should just stay on this chopper and fly home," Samson says. He does not like going into a mission blind. He needs not only an objective but also a reason for risking his life.

"I got a feeling they won't let us." Roscoe looks at Samson.

"You are right. We have been drafted."

The chopper lands, and a soldier quickly yanks the door open. All four climb out. The soldier tells them not to worry about their gear. Samson watches a small group of heavily armed soldiers move toward two choppers. Once again, he frowns. "That's the Thirty-third. What the hell are they doing here?"

"They're going up," Roscoe says, watching the men. "The easy way. If they can fly up, why can't we?"

"Why do I have a feeling we are in a life-threatening situation?" Yoshiko says.

"Now or later?" Roscoe asks.

"All the same if you ask me," Samson says. "Those soldiers are the guys whose faces you never see on TV."

"I got one of my feelings. We should just make a run for it." Roscoe says

"I am right there with you," Samson says. "But they have guns."

"Too many guns if you ask me."

"Too many for a crashed plane."

CHAPTER 13

FAR FROM HOME

Commander stands in the middle of a room shaped like an octagon. He is now wearing a more casual uniform. It's more like a dark blue jumpsuit with a gold braid.

Four workstations are manned by aliens. Three large and several smaller monitors fill the three walls at the front of the room. An elevator occupies the last wall. Two aliens in black uniforms stand by it.

Flashing red lights give the bridge an eerie look. The monitors provide different mountain views, but they are pretty fuzzy. The smaller ones blink on and off.

Commander remains calm on the outside. Inside, he has too many questions. Most can be answered. One thing he is sure of is that it was no accident. They ended up on this planet. It is outside the jurisdiction of any other planet. It really was of no interest to his and most worlds. A few planets sent research teams. He has heard the stories about these beings called Earthlings. Savages, in his mind - and he is a solider. Bad luck is not the reason they landed here. There is a fortune down in the ship's vaults. He and his crew could be wiped out, and no one would wonder what happened. But first, he had to deal with the Earthlings. The elevator opens halfway. Captain shoves the doors back. The Colonel follows her over to Commander. The Colonel is dressed in a white jumpsuit. Captain is dressed in her battle uniform, with a pistol on her hip and a rifle in her hand.

"Stans report?" Commander asks.

"We have limited power," Colonel says.

"I can see that. Is the core damaged?" Commander snaps, glaring at the Colonel.

"No, it seems to be operating at full power, and there appear to be no leaks."

"I assume you checked the Questor Channeler?"

"That was the first thing I checked. It is functioning normally. Commander, I am not a technician..."

"Don't tell what you are not. Tell me what you have been doing for the last twenty-six hours."

"Commander, I..." the Colonel starts to say.

"Don't you dare say you are not a technician," Captain growls.

"I suggest you figure out what it is before the Earthling's helicopters start landing," Commander says calmly.

"Commander, it has been over twenty hours." Captain asks, "What do you think is keeping them?"

"I picked this landing spot because it is a hard-to-reach location," he says, watching the flickering monitors. "Or they are being cautious. We did collide with two of their ships. They will consider this a hostile act."

"Perhaps they don't know where we are?" Colonel says. We could negotiate with them.

"How did you ever get to be a Colonel..?" Captain asks with genuine curiosity.

"Captain! I am your superior officer..."

"Colonel!" Commander says, but for the first time, shows a little anger. "Go to Engineering and get this ship up and running because if you don't, I will personally throw you off this mountain."

Colonel salutes and quickly leaves the bridge. They watch him go and then return their attention to the monitors. Captain looks around the bridge.

"Be careful, Colonel has friends. We need to get off this planet as quickly as possible," Commander says.

"Commander, we both know the Earthlings are coming. What do you plan to do when they arrive?" Captain says in a challenging tone.

"They cannot take this ship. I will self-destruct it before that happens. We can't let these Earthlings take us alive," Commander says with a deep sigh. "They have used their probes and aircraft to get images of us. The next step will be to send up an armed response. Their goal will be to take the ship and kill us if necessary."

"That will not happen," Captain says with ice in her voice.

"You will deal with them as I ordered. You will have the advantage. They won't expect us to fight back. It is the second team I am interested in. They will want to get a closer look at the ship. Take more images. If we are lucky, they will send up what they call a scientist. One who has a history with ships of our type? They could decide to use their aircraft to just destroy the top of this mountain top."

"We have the weaponry to deal with their slow-moving aircraft."

"I wish to avoid any more carnage. The fact is, we can only stay on top of this mountain for a while. As the Earthlings say, the clock is ticking."

CHAPTER 14

THIS ONE IS DIFFERENT

Ryan sat with his men in the back of the chopper. He could feel the tension not only in his men but himself. This was not his first encounter with extraterrestrials. So far, he had only encountered what the men called *bubble heads* and *greys*. Most were dead because their crafts had crashed. Some were severely injured, dying soon after. Occasionally, they caught one or two alive. They had no psychic powers. They just gave up and meekly followed their capturers. He never knew what happened to them and didn't want to know. He would like to think they were treated well at Base 994, not at Dreamland, Aka Area 51. Two days after that crash in 1947, what they found, including the bodies, was moved to a new location. Ryan wasn't exactly sure where it was. He doesn't want to know. Ryan had to hand over whatever they found to whoever was in charge; they did a hell of a job convincing everyone. Roswell was where all the action was. He wonders who the Deacon answers to.

Another thing he doesn't want to know.

He nods to his men. "Get ready."

This feels different. The thing is shaped like a saucer, but what looks like turrets are mounted on the top. Weapons. For some reason, it looks sleeker than the other ones Ryan has found. Every bone in his body to*ld him that these were soldiers.* They *had* taken out two F-16.

The chopper comes down within a foot of the mountaintop. Ryan barks for his men to get out. He jumps out last and studies the area. He can barely see anything. Black rocks and snow are being whipped around. Ryan realizes this is his first time on a really high mountain. He didn't climb it, so it's nothing to brag about. "All right, move out. Stay sharp."

An older man with stripes on his shoulders says in a harsh whisper, "You heard the man! Watson, you take point. Anderson, watch the back door. Stay on your toes."

The soldiers move out. Ryan brings up the rear. He motions the radio man over, who hands him the mic.

"Black Bird to Ground Star. We are on the ground and moving toward our objective."

Ryan hands back the radio and follows his men, praying but not believing whoever these guys are had no idea they were there.

Captain watches the troops with a futuristic scope. There is a hint of a smile on her lips as she watches. Commander comes up and taps her shoulder. "Report."

"They are fully armed and appear somewhat organized," Captain says. "Their formation is effective but somewhat sloppy. Most of them look afraid. Orders, sir?"

"They came to fight," Commander says, taking out the scope and looking through it. "Let's give them one."

"I mean no disrespect, Commander; I do not see how killing these men gets us off this planet. It will confirm their suspicions about us. "

Commander lowers the scope and smiles. "Who said anything about killing? Set weapons on stun. Then, take their weapons. They will have to return to their base. This will confuse them. We are just buying time and hoping they send up a scientist."

"And if they don't?"

"Captain, I have told you before. One problem at a time."

Ryan has moved to the head of his men. They are crossing a narrow area and must move a single file. The passage is surrounded by jagged rocks. Ryan puts his fist up. The men stop. He can feel them. "DOWN!"

The command comes too late. Dozens of yellow laser beams start to hit the men. Ryan goes down first. The battle is over before it ever began.

Captain walks up and studies the stunned soldiers. She looks up as her men approach. "Secure the area! Move it! Let's make sure we have them all. Take their weapons...and their jackets."

Captain wanders around the soldiers, watching her men take the weapons and jackets. She stops by the stunned radioman and smiles, kneeling and picking up the mic. "Hello. Hello."

A crackly voice comes out, "Identify yourself."

"I don't think that will be necessary. The men you set up need to be picked up. It is freezing up here. I will leave this device on so you can pick them up. We will be watching. No one will leave this mountain if you do anything but pick up these men."

"Who is this?"

Captain, annoyed, tosses down the mic.

Commander walks up and studies the battle area. He kneels down and fingers a coil of rope attached to one of the soldiers' packs. He looks toward the mountain's edge. "I want four teams on constant patrol to watch the mountain face."

"May I ask what they are watching for?" Captain asks.

"The next group may come in the next aircraft. But they may try to climb the mountain. I have read that they climb mountains on this planet."

"I find it hard to believe they would try to climb this one."

"It is my understanding there are men and women on this planet who would climb this mountain just for fun."

"Really," Captain says, looking toward the end of the cliff. "That would be a person worth meeting."

CHAPTER 15

SETTING THE CLOCK

Deacon sits at the table. He has been studying the photos and reports. The voice on the radio makes them look up. It was female. That, he found interesting. It would be their first encounter with a female. What kind of female? This is a whole new alien. They had demonstrated surrendering wasn't an option. They had taken out the entire squad.

Parker has been standing by the radio. The man working it is fiddling with the dials. "I am only getting static, sir."

The general goes to the flap and looks up the mountain. He turns and throws down his cigar stub. "I think it's time to accept the obvious."

"And that would be?" Deacon asks in his usual calm voice.

"Ryan and his men are dead."

"That is not the impression I got. It sounded like our friends wanted us to pick up the wounded. I suggest we do that."

"They've never fought back before. This is a trap. They want to take out our choppers and more men."

"General, I think you are letting your emotions get the better of you..."

"Base! Base!" Ryan's voice comes over the radio. "Ryan here. All men are down but alive. They took our weapons and jackets. We need to be picked up now. Base, can you hear me?!"

"They're alive!" Parker gasps and runs to the radio. He grabs the mic. "Ryan, is the area secure?"

"As far as I can tell. Sir, they had every chance to kill us or take us prisoner. They didn't. Took our weapons and jackets. We are unarmed and freezing. Pick us up."

"They are on the way," Parker says. He tosses the mic to the radio operator. "Get our people off that mountain. They didn't kill them."

"Makes one wonder what they'll do next," Deacon muses. He watches the radio operator order the choppers.

"I don't intend to find out. I'm calling in a full-air strike," Parker says, pulling out another cigar.

"General, I was hoping we could do something more subtle."

"Subtle, hell! I will blow that thing to hell before they do anything else."

"Just what do you think they are doing?"

"Stalling. They are buying time. This could be a scout ship. They could be sending a signal back to their main fleet."

"Let's take a moment to calm down. Why not kill our men if this were an invading force."

"Why else would they be here? On top of a mountain?"

"I can think of several possibilities," Deacon says, then lets off a long sigh. "General, let's remember the protocol. It is now my mission."

"Deacon, the longer we wait, the deeper they get dug in."

"Dug in. On top of a mountain. Surrounded by our troops."

"They are a threat."

"Aren't you the least bit curious?"

"We both know what's up there. You've been collecting bits and pieces for years."

"Bits and pieces. Now, we finally have the opportunity to get one fully intact, or at least get a closer look. Perhaps we can even communicate with them. Bombing the site is overreacting, and I will put that in my report."

"You want to put the world at risk just so you can get some pictures?"

"I am not entirely convinced the world is at risk. Compromise. Just give me forty-eight hours." Deacon says.

"I'll give you twelve."

"Twenty-four."

"I'll give you twenty."

"Twenty it is."

"You better get going. The clock is ticking."

"General, the clock has been ticking since our friends landed."

CHAPTER 16

Deacon sits behind a card table, looking through photos of dead aliens. They all look like the typical gray aliens with black eyes. He puts these down and opens a file with Roscoe's picture. The second one has a picture of Yoshiko.

Brett slumps into a chair, looking more like a moody teenager than a spy. Deacon doesn't even look up. "Watershaw was a valuable operative. His family is already asking questions."

"I got you what you wanted!" Brett snaps, sitting up.

"You exceeded orders. Once again. You think the results justify your methods. They do not. You have cost me three operatives in less than a year."

"But completed every mission."

"You remind me of a bull in a china shop. Interesting to watch but too costly in the long run. On the other hand, MythBusters proved that saying to be in error," Deacon says with a rare smile. "The only reasons you are here are because you have the needed clearance and your relationship with Roscoe. Which I now believe to be on thin ice."

"Yet he is here, and so am I."

For the first time, Deacon looks annoyed. Then he speaks very slowly: "You have a Nobel Peace Prize-winning scientist and a world-class mountain climber who is a legend. If something were to happen to them, people would start to ask questions I have no desire to answer. You understand?"

"I will get them back."

"You'll do more than that. I want the whole team back in one piece. This is a simple recon mission. You go up, find the objective, and take pictures. Then leave."

Brett rises and picks up one of the pictures. He glances at it and tosses it down. "Do we know who's up there?"

"No," Deacon says. "It is not our grey-skinned friends. These are different. They're shooting back. They just wiped out the Thirty-Third. No, this is the important thing: they haven't killed anyone." Deacon smiles. "They actually radioed us to come and get our men. I am very interested in these visitors. I believe now the planes were an accident. You and Samson are there to protect Roscoe and the good doctor. Am I understood?"

"What if we get caught?"

"I just told you. The visitors seem to be reluctant to kill. I am going to show them the same courtesy. In nineteen hours and fifty-four minutes, the Army will drop little bundles of joy on the top of that mountain. I suggest you don't get caught."

"What if the opportunity arises to take the ship or capture a crew member?"

Looking more than annoyed, he once again speaks very slowly. "If the opportunity arises, Dr. Sasaki and Roscoe are in no danger."

"What if it comes down to Sasaki, Roscoe, or the ship?"

"Why do you always have to push me?"

"It's just my nature."

"If Roscoe and Dr. Sasaki come to any harm, I suggest you stay on top of that mountain and try to use that flying saucer to escape." Deacon's voice grows louder. "Do we understand each other?"

"You got it," Brett says in a less-than-convincing tone.

"Say it!" Deacon almost shouts. "Say *I will follow orders*. Say it."

"I will follow orders. Roscoe and Sasaki back safely."

"One more thing," Deacon says, sitting down. "Dr. Halley said you missed your appointment."

"I was still in the field."

"No, you weren't. Our policy is that all agents have a complete physical and psychiatric evaluation at least once a year. When you come down that mountain, you will go see Dr. Halley. Unless you wish to be retired."

"I don't react well to threats."

"Brett, you are forgetting who you are talking to and what I am capable of. I don't care how you react to this. See the doctor, or I will retire you."

Brett gives Deacon a cold stare. Deacon is more amused than threatened. Deacon smiles and goes back to his files. It is obvious who the bigger threat is.

CHAPTER 17

NEED TO KNOW

Roscoe sits on a crate, carefully checking his climbing gear. Samson walks in and begins to wander around the tent while he studies the climber. "Time for our briefing."

"I'll be right there," Roscoe says without looking up. Samson continues to study Roscoe. He finally looks up. "What?"

"Just wondering why you haven't climbed since you fell off that mountain."

"Everyone seems to want to know," Roscoe says. "The last one was this beautiful redhead. I told her, but that was after a night that I will always remember. That's not an option with you."

Samson keeps staring.

"Let me guess. You think I've lost my nerve."

"Thought has crossed my mind. That's the third time you've checked your equipment."

"You ever climb a mountain?"

"A couple in California during my training."

"I bet it was summer; the weather was terrific. There was no wind. It took you less than an hour, maybe two."

"Hour and a half. Your point?"

"We are about to climb a mountain rated an easy 5. Which means it is a bitch to climb in good weather. Plus, we are doing it at the crack of dawn. I have no idea what your skill set is or the good doctor's. Brett is not as good as he thinks he is. A storm will likely hit before we reach the top. So you'll excuse me for being a little careful."

"So why haven't you climbed?" Samson tries to sound more intimidating.

"I retired. I lost my nerve. It's none of your business. Pick any reason you want. I've got a feeling no matter what I say, you're still not going to like me."

"You got that right, hot shot."

"Then I'll make you like me even less. That cold front is coming faster, so we could face rain, sleet, and snow mixed with high winds."

"Trying to scare me? It ain't working."

"That's unfortunate. We have six hours to climb a mountain that takes eight in good weather."

"You're going to get me killed."

"We will die together. Won't that be fun?" Roscoe suddenly gets serious. "You are an amateur climber about to climb a mountain that scares most pros. If anyone gets you killed up there, it'll be you. I just pray you don't take me with you."

"I hope you climb as good as you talk."

Samson walks out. Roscoe begins to wrap a rope. "Yeah, I talk real good."

Deacon sits at his table, sipping coffee. Yoshiko sits on a cot, drinking coffee and nibbling on a Danish. Samson and Brett are slumped in two chairs. Roscoe comes in but stays by the tent flap.

"Ah, Roscoe. Better late than never," Deacon says.

"Better any place than here, but what the hey." Roscoe walks to the coffee pot and pours himself a cup. He spots the Danish in Yoshiko's hand. "Where did you get that?"

"The mess tent," Yoshiko says with a smile.

"We will get you a Danish later." Deacon motions to the cot. Roscoe stays standing and sips his coffee. "I cannot stress the importance of time in the operation. I have been informed the storm front is coming in faster than expected, so we are up against the clock."

"What is the mission? Exactly why are we here?" Roscoe asks.

"Sorry, that's on a need-to-know basis. You simply have to get our people up the mountain and back down."

"Well...it's Deacon, right?" Roscoe points his finger at the man. "Before I risk my butt for you, I need to know."

"Roscoe," Brett says, giving a cold look.

"When I first arrived, I saw four choppers take off full of heavily armed soldiers. Samson seemed to think they were pretty tough guys."

"No argument here." Samson almost smiles. "Please continue."

"A short time later, I heard a strange noise coming from the mountain. Not gunfire. Strange noises, like the ones you hear in Star Wars movies. The reason I was late is because I saw these same choppers come back. Medics and other soldiers were helping these very tough soldiers out and over to the field hospital. Oddly, they had no weapons or jackets. Which could explain why they looked half-frozen. So tell me what is happening, or get yourself another boy."

"I hate to admit it, but the man has a point," Samson says.

"I agree," Yoshiko says. "I hope I haven't been called here for a plane crash because I would be no help."

"Looks like we all need to know," Roscoe says, looking at Deacon.

Deacon studies the group and looks at Roscoe. Brett just shrugs. "An unidentified object has crashed or landed on top of the mountain. We believe it to be a real flying saucer."

"A flying saucer?" Roscoe asks.

"Its occupants are apparently hostile. Two planes were taken down. The Thirty-Third was taken out, although not killed, by some sort of laser weapon that stunned them."

"A flying saucer?" Roscoe asks again.

"The military plans to bomb the site in nineteen hours and forty-three minutes," Deacon says in a calm tone.

"Do you have photos?" Yoshiko asks, sitting up now, very interested.

Deacon hands her several photos.

She studies them.

"The weather makes clearer shots impossible."

"This is bigger than anything I have heard of. The design is slightly different. These turrets on top could be weapons. We could be dealing with a military craft."

"That is General Parker's option, hence his decision to bomb the site. I also believe it is a military craft, but their reluctance to kill gives me pause. It could be that taking out the planes was an accident. Still, you must be extremely cautious. Roscoe, what face are you planning to climb?"

"A real flying saucer?" Roscoe asks again.

"Roscoe, deal with it," Brett snaps.

Roscoe looks unhappy and then says, "The west face."

"That's the hardest face. Has it been done before at this time of the year?" Deacon asks.

"A couple dozen times."

"How difficult are we talking about?" Deacon asks.

"The first snow has already fallen." Roscoe sips his coffee. "The glacier isn't melting, and the wind is dying down. So it could be worse. The real worry is the cold front moving in."

"The other team members have limited climbing experience."

"It's better than no experience." Samson looks at Roscoe, who just smiles at him.

"Wouldn't the south face be easier?" Deacon asks.

"It would be a cakewalk, but it would take us fourteen hours. We got ten. Look, if they do as I say, they should be fine. They all have some climbing experience."

"West face it is."

"Isn't the west face almost straight up?" Brett asks.

"Yes, that is what makes it faster," Roscoe says.

"I hope you're as good as they say you are." Yoshiko smiles.

"Trust me. I'm the best."

"I wouldn't trust you to help me climb a ladder," Samson says.

"Stay behind." He smiles at Yoshiko. It will be more fun just with the doctor."

Samson starts to get up, but Brett's hand stops him. He pats Samson's arm and says, "Trust me. He is the best."

Deacon watches the men and clears his throat. "We now have nineteen hours and thirty-seven minutes. I suggest you leave at once."

Brett quickly leaves. Yoshiko gets up and goes to Roscoe. "Would you mind checking out my equipment?"

"Nothing I like better," Roscoe says. "Better safe than sorry."

They walk out together. Samson stands up. Deacon looks up from his papers. "Samson, a minute of your time."

Samson is good at reading faces. This talent has saved his life more than once. "Do we have a problem?"

"Let's just say I want to keep the body count down."

CHAPTER 18

PROBLEMS WITH PITONS AND EXPLOSIVES

A helicopter lands close to the base of the mountain. The four all climb out. Roscoe is now wearing a bright orange and black jacket with a matching climbing bib, pants, and boots. Yoshika is dressed in black and red. Both Brett and Samson are wearing black and white camo winter gear. A crewman hands out all the packs to Roscoe. He frowns when the last two packs are given to him. He takes them away from the chopper and looks at the others. "Stretch your muscles."

They are stretching while Roscoe begins to open the two packs. Brett looks over. "Hey, what are you doing?"

"Your packs are too heavy. No unnecessary gear."

Roscoe pulls out a block of plastic explosives. He rolls it around in his hands and looks. Samson comes over and looks at it. "What the hell is this?"

Samson kneels down and takes out another block. "Explosives."

Yoshiko comes over and looks down. "I know that stuff. It is a very powerful plastic explosive."

"I like to be prepared," Brett says, looking defensive.

"For what? We're just supposed to sneak up and take pictures," she says, offended by his actions.

The chopper's engine roars to life. The blades spin faster and faster, sending snow everywhere. The team is forced to cover their faces. It flies off into the dull morning sky. Roscoe lets off an angry sigh. "Lady and gentlemen, it's a moot point. I assume we just can't leave it here."

Roscoe tosses the block to Brett with a cool glare and finally says, "I should walk away right now."

"But you won't," Brett says, trying to be charming.

"Don't push me. As of this moment, we are no longer friends." He moves to Samson's pack and pulls out a bunch of steel pitons. "Pitons?"

"Even an amateur like me knows we need pitons to climb a mountain like that," Samson says with a smile.

"Uh-ho." Yoshiko smiles like she knows the problem.

"I don't use pitons. I hate pitons. I use friends." Roscoe goes to his pack and pulls out a bunch of metal half-circle devices connected with axles. Roscoe holds up one round metal device. It clicks wider. "It has been discovered slamming metal spikes into a mountain face causes damage to the rock. Over time, pitons can do real damage to a mountain overall. These just slip into a crack, and bingo. A rope hold. Plus, easy to pull out."

Roscoe throws down the pitons in the snow. "Savage. You can bring them, but I won't use them. Leave them behind. Less weight for you to carry."

Roscoe looks up at the sky. He turns to the group and up at the mountain. "Are you going to be a bitch today or play nice? Let's move. The storm's coming in."

Brett takes a pistol, pulls out the mag, checks it, and slams it back. He pulls back the slide and lets it go back with a loud *click*. "I'm ready."

"For what? The mountain may kill us, but I guarantee it won't mug us."

Samson picks up the pitons, looks at the mountain, and drops them. "I'll pick these up on the way back."

The soldier pulls on his pack but keeps his eyes on Brett. Roscoe pulls on his pack and moves off. Yoshiko follows. Brett puts away the pistol and looks at Samson.

"After you. I'll bring up the rear," Samson says.

Brett just smiles and trots off after the others. Samson takes out his pistol, checks it, and puts it away.

After a brief hike up, the group comes to the base. The gray and black rock wall seems to reach up into the sky. The top is covered by clouds. Roscoe pulls off his pack and takes out four French rolls and four bars of chocolate. He starts to hand them out. "Take, eat. I promise, halfway up the mountain, you'll thank me."

They take the rolls and candy. Roscoe munches on a roll while studying the mountain as he pulls on his harness. In his mind, he think*s that every climb is different. You can climb the same mountain a dozen times and encounter different problems every time. Just because the mountain didn't kill you last time. It doesn't mean it won't kill you this time.*

Roscoe removes his glove, reaches out, and touches the cold stone. He runs his hand over it like he's trying to feel the mountain. The climber looks up and smiles. "Good to see you too, baby."

"What do you think?" Yoshiko asks, coming up beside him.

"I think she is in a good mood. All right, sweetheart. Let's dance." Roscoe pulls a coiled rope around his upper body. Then, he attaches the rope, friends, and ice ax to his harness. He hands the end of the rope to Yoshiko, who clips it to her harness. "Obviously, I will lead. Then Yoshiko, Samson. Brett brings up the rear. Let's be respectful and careful. All right, people, our mountain is ready. Are you?"

Roscoe grabs hold of a rock and pulls himself up. As he finds holds and moves up the mountain, he is obviously very good.

"What do you know, he can climb?" Samson says.

CHAPTER 19

LOST FRIENDS

Roscoe is flat against the mountain, his face pressed against the icy cold stone. The tips of his boots are resting on a very thin outcrop. One hand has a good grip on a hole in the side of the cliff; his other, pressed against the rock, slowly inches up. Roscoe's eyes are closed as he feels his way up the cliff. He tries to remember the last time he came this way. Surprisingly, he is not nervous. He is in his element. He has climbed this mountain before. More than once. He knows a hold somewhere above him, a crevasse big enough to fit in a friend. The wind blows him against the hard rock, but the mountain pushes back.

Every mountain climber knows gravity is a bitch.

In his mind, he keeps telling himself the crevasse is there. Someone yells, "How are you doing?" He ignores them while telling himself never to climb with rookies again.

Suddenly, his fingers slip into an opening. His eyes pop open, a smile coming to his face. He uses his hand to sweep out any debris, then slowly reaches down and takes a friend off his harness. This time, he strains up to push the device into the crack. Once in, he clicks it open. After snapping on a clip, he snaps in the rope. Roscoe uses this as a handhold as he looks up. "Okay, there should be a ledge up there."

His eyes study the face. There is another outcrop just up to the left of his hand. His glove tightens around the slip. Once again, he studies the face and takes a breath before pushing up with his legs. For a brief second, only his right hand supports him. His hands grab the outcrop while his feet dance around, looking for any hold. His left boot finds something. Roscoe doesn't care what it is. It just gives more support. He brings up his right boot and finds another hold. The climber pushes up and finds another hold. Slowly, he works his way up a ledge. Roscoe pulls himself onto the rock, and slumps face down, panting. "Yeah, piece of cake."

"Are you okay?" someone yells.

"No, I am not. I should be in sunny California with Charlie," Roscoe mutters as he sits up and braces against the mountain. He gets a tight grip on the rope. "Instead, I am here. Freezing my butt off and climbing a mountain to fight aliens who probably want to do all kinds of nasty things to me. COME UP!"

The rope tightens. A couple minutes later, Yoshiko climbs onto the ledge and sits by Roscoe. He looks at her. "Great view."

"Me or the mountains?" she asks drily.

"Both. You're excellent. So what else do you do? When you are not hunting aliens."

"I teach. Which I hate. I do government-funded research at a university."

"They give you a lot of money to risk your life occasionally?"

"It's never been dangerous before. Sometimes, I get called to UFO crash sites and spend two or three weeks picking up the pieces, then try to put it back together."

"Sounds like interesting work. Married?"

"Only to my job. Not interested. You're nice, but I have you pegged as a guy, not into relationships. Please don't say you haven't met the right woman."

"Damn, it was just on the tip of my tongue."

"Whenever you're ready!" Brett yells.

Yoshiko braces herself against the mountain while Roscoe gets up and studies the cliff. She yells, "Ready! And we're making good time."

"We were. The storm is moving in faster than I thought. We better move our butts." Roscoe tests a few handholds.

Samson climbs up onto the ledge and braces himself. "Ready."

"You get Brett up while I figure out our next move," Roscoe says as he tries different holds on the face. A few moments later, Brett climbs up onto the ledge. He slumps down, breathing really hard. Roscoe looks down at Brett. Samson and he exchange a smile. "You want safe or fast?"

"I prefer both, but we're fighting the clock." Brett struggles up into a sitting position. He wipes the sweat off his face and takes a long drink from his water bottle.

"Straight up, we save two hours. Of course, it's a little dangerous."

"Do it," Brett says as he rubs his arms and shoulders. Samson is doing the same.

"Feel muscles that you never knew you had?" Roscoe asks.

Smiling, Samson says, "Shouldn't you be climbing or something? By the way, could you keep the chatter down? We do have hostiles above us."

"Yes, I have no interest in being probed. Brett, give me the friends you picked up."

Brett hands him three friends. Roscoe stares at them.

"Brett, bringing up the rear means you collect the friends. All of them."

"Sorry, I didn't get them all. I was more concerned with holding on than collecting your stupid friends."

Roscoe glares at him. "I told you weren't ready for this climb. We're now short on friends."

Yoshiko pulls off her pack and digs inside. She brings out a bunch of friends and holds them up. Roscoe takes them and begins to attach them to his harness. "Thank you. Yoshiko, switch places with Brett."

"You want her to bring up the rear?" Brett says, looking shocked.

"Yes, I do. Let me give you guys a news flash: I don't think I got enough of these beauties to get us to the top."

"I thought you could climb this thing without ropes?" Samson asked.

"I can. You want to try?"

"No, thank you. You're the expert."

"Look, I'll do better." Brett stands up. "The fact is, I'm a little more experienced than Yoshiko.

"God, you will get over it." Roscoe exchanges rope between Brett and Yoshiko. "Ego has no place in mountain climbing. Brett, no offense, but the lady can climb circles around you. Besides, it wasn't a request; it was an order. Remember, I'm in charge until we reach the top. Unless you want to take over. I can make my way down."

The two men stare at each other. Roscoe laughs and starts to climb up the face.

CHAPTER 20

YOU GOT TO LOVE GRAVITY...NOT

Roscoe is climbing the face of the mountain. There are few holds, and it is slow going. He stops to get his bearings. The cliff is straight up, with what looks like very few holds. "Okay, bright boy, now what?"

Roscoe reaches up and feels around the cliff. He actually slumps against the cliff. Frustrated, he looks down. "Yoshiko! I can't find a hold. Do you see anything above me?"

Yoshiko and the others are still on the small ledge. Brett is sitting but looking up. Samson is watching with his arms folded, smiling a little. Yoshiko studies the cliff face and frowns. "There is a small crevice just above your hand."

"Why can't it ever be easy? If it was easy, everyone would be doing it." Roscoe hangs onto the face for a moment. He brings up his foot to another rock and tests it. Roscoe pushes himself up and reaches for the crevice. The rock starts to give way. Roscoe feels it going and grabs onto another rock. The rock falls away, leaving Roscoe hanging by his hands.

Brett sees this and jumps up. "I got you!"

"I'm not falling...yet!"

Roscoe tries to find holds for his feet but can't find one. He slowly pulls himself up to the crevice and quickly grabs another handhold. Roscoe is panting and sweating heavily as he finally finds another foothold.

Yoshiko and the others watch with concern. She rubs her hands together and yells, "You okay?"

"Wonderful. I just stopped to take in the view," Roscoe says, more to himself than Yoshiko. He is holding onto the rock while studying the face.

"I'm impressed," Samson says, leaning out for a better view.

"Why don't you tell him that to his face?" Yoshiko asks, looking up at the much bigger man.

"His ego is big enough."

Roscoe begins to climb again until he reaches a small ledge. He sits back and rests for a second. Roscoe looks at his rope and tugs it a couple times. He rubs it with his thumbs. He sits back, looks up, and then nods. "Yo! I don't like the look of my rope. Send me up a new one!"

"On the way!" Yoshiko yells.

Brett unclips himself from Roscoe's line and pulls a coil of rope off his shoulder. He ties it to the other rope and tugs on the line. Roscoe pulls up the rope. He stops when a cracking sound begins. Suddenly, the ledge gives way. The group ducks the falling rocks and watches Roscoe fall past them. He bangs against the mountain and snags a hold with one hand. He desperately looks for another hold. His feet find a small outcrop. This lets him see another hand grip.

The group looks down at him with concern.

"Are you okay?" Brett asks.

"Stop asking me that! I am not okay!"

Samson quickly grabs a coil of rope and throws one end down to him. Roscoe catches the rope. "Thank you."

Samson smiles but suddenly realizes the other end isn't secure. The whole rope goes over the edge. Roscoe watches the rope fall by him. He presses his face against the rock and groans. "Hey guys, you're supposed to keep one end."

"Don't worry, we'll get you up!" Brett yells.

"I'm a dead man. I will never again climb...with amateurs.

Brett looks over the edge and yells, "Throw up the other end."

Roscoe looks at the rope and shakes his head. He looks up and drops the ropes. Then, a low, crumbling sound comes from above. "ROCKS!"

"What?!" Brett asked.

"Sounded like locks?" Samson said.

"Falling rocks!" Yoshiko yells, looking up.

They quickly press themselves against the mountain face, avoiding the falling rocks. Roscoe is not as lucky, as a few of the small ones bounce off him. He drops the rope and uses his free arm to cover his head.

"Give me the other rope. I'm going down," Brett says.

"I don't think that is a good idea," Yoshiko says.

Samson says, "I thought he could climb without help?"

Roscoe watches them argue. He begins to climb the face without a rope. It's actually easier this time since he just climbed it.

"He may be hurt," Yoshiko says.

"Well, that's just great," Samson says. "If he is hurt, how do we get to the top?"

Roscoe continues to climb up and manages to pull himself onto the ledge. He watches them argue. The others realize he is up and kneel down.

"You okay?" Brett asks.

"You hurt?" Yoshiko asks with concern.

"I hate you all." Roscoe climbs to his feet. Samson hands him the rope he was carrying. Roscoe snaps it onto his harness. "Hook yourselves up. Sorry. I still like you." Roscoe smiles at Yoshiko

"Thank you so much," Yoshiko says. "I still won't go out with you."

"Ouch," Samson says.

CHAPTER 21

STILL HATING PITONS

Roscoe is working his way over the overhang. He puts a friend into a hole and clicks a rope into it. Roscoe continues to do this until he is hanging under the ledge. The rope and his hands are the only things keeping him from falling. He reaches for another friend, but his belt is empty. "Okay, can't go back..."

Roscoe looks around and spots a piton in the rock. It looks old and rusted. He smiles and looks up to the heavens. "Thank you.”

He pulls himself up and clips his rope onto the piton. It holds. "Now, let's hope you defaced the cliff all the way up.”

Roscoe finds another one and moves up to it. It looks just as bad as the other one. "Whoever you are, I love you.”

He hooks up his rope and moves on. He is now just about to come around the ledge. The last piton comes out, quickly followed by a second one. Roscoe finds himself hanging upside down in mid-air. "I hate this!”

Roscoe twists around, trying to get a hold of any kind. He twirls around. His helmet bangs against the rock. He manages to get one hand on the cliff and pull himself upright. "Don't panic. We've done this before.”

He pulls himself up the rock and grabs onto a small outcrop.

“Almost there. We can do this. Just stay calm.”

Roscoe begins to climb over the overhang without using rope, grunting and sweating as he slowly moves up the mountain. "Yes. We are cookin.'”

He is almost at the top when it begins to snow. He looks up. "Really?"

Roscoe grabs the cliff edge and pulls himself up onto the top. He then falls back on the ledge and tries to catch his breath while the snow falls.

"Are you okay?" Yoshiko yells.

Roscoe looks up into the dark sky. "Please stop asking me that."

CHAPTER 22

CLOSE ENCOUNTER OF THE WORST KIND

Captain watches Roscoe help Yoshiko up through her scope. A group of soldiers stands behind her. The scope is lowered, revealing her face. She looks impressed. "They actually did it. They climbed up the side of this mountain."

"Is that possible?" one of the soldiers asks.

"Apparently so. There the Earthlings are. Get the Commander. Remember, we want them alive."

The snow is falling a little heavier now. Roscoe has set up a small camp stove and is making coffee while watching the others get ready. Samson and Brett are checking their weapons. Yoshiko is checking a video camera. She hands this to Brett. "You do video."

"What?" Brett asks, looking annoyed, but takes the camera. "Why me?"

"You're a spy. I assume you have taken pictures under similar circumstances." Yoshiko looks at him as she checks another camera. Then she checks what looks like a TV remote. It beeps softly. "Okay, no sign of radiation...yet."

Brett moves away from the others and looks ahead, but the snow makes it difficult. "We're not too far away. I figure just over that ridge."

"They can spot that fire a mile away," Samson says, kneeling down.

"You really think they don't know we are here?" Roscoe asks.

"Good point. Watch yourself."

"You ready, doctor?"

Yoshiko looks at Roscoe. "You're not coming?"

"They've already shown themselves to be unfriendly. I'll pass." Roscoe says, smiling. "Besides, my coffee is almost ready."

"Best he stays here. We may have to leave in a hurry," Samson says.

"I'll be ready. Going down will be a little easier."

"Roscoe," Samson says.

"I know, I'm wonderful, and you are amazed by how great a climber I am."

"Jerk."

"You be careful out there."

"I'm always careful."

Brett and Yoshiko walk off. Samson starts to walk off but comes back when Roscoe calls him back. "Brett has always been a little crazy," Roscoe says, "but I think he might be close to the edge. Don't turn your back on him."

"You may need this. Just in case." Samson pulls his pack out and removes a small pistol.

"I haven't fired one in years."

"It's just like riding a bike. It'll come back to you."

Roscoe takes the pistol and checks it, looking like he has some experience with a gun.

"The clip holds fifteen. Count your shots."

Samson walks off. Roscoe pours coffee, sits back, and plays fast draw with the pistol.

Captain smiles as she lowers her scope. Commander comes up and takes the scope. He watches the group: "Just the four."

"Yes, sir. I think you were right," Captain says. "I think it's some kind of reconnaissance team. The woman is carrying some kind of photo device."

"The woman doesn't look like a soldier," Commander says, looking through the scope again. "She could be a tech or a scientist. Give them some room. Let's see what they do. Get a unit behind them."

They move across the slope but stop. All the soldiers' jackets are piled in one spot. There is no sign of the weapons or packs. Brett pulls out his night scope and looks ahead.

"Stay frosty. Which way?" Samson asks.

"Just over that snowbank," Brett says. "I can see one of the turrets. They are definitely weapons."

Brett motions the group forward. They come to the snow back, drop down, and crawl until they can peek over it. Yoshiko's eyes become huge as she takes in the silver, gold, and black disc. She begins to take pictures as fast as she can. "This is amazing. Brett, don't just lie there. Get some videos."

Brett glances at her. He pulls out the video camera and points it over the ridge. Yoshiko puts down her camera, pulls out her journal, and takes quick notes. She puts away the journal and pulls out a nightscope. "We have to get closer."

"Doc, this is as close as we are going to get," Samson says.

Suddenly, yellow laser blasts tear the ground apart. Captain and her soldiers rush out behind some boulders, helmets on, and visors down. Both Samson and Brett cling to their weapons, unsure what to do.

"I have orders to take you alive. The choice is yours," Captain says.

Samson looks behind him as another group of soldiers approach. They take up positions with weapons ready.

"We choose to live." Samson slowly stands, drops his weapons, and puts up his hands. Brett follows his lead. Yoshiko puts down her night scope and stands up. Captain's men surround them and pick up the weapons. The alien soldiers push up their visors. Samson's mouth drops open at the sight of the green-tinted aliens with purple eyes. Yoshiko's eyes are as big as saucers as she moves right up to one of the soldiers and gives him a good look. Brett just stands there.

"My God, you're beautiful," she says, looking amazed. "You are nothing like I expected. You are so similar to us in appearance."

The alien isn't sure what to do with Yoshiko as he pushes her into line with Samson and Brett. The Captain walks up and looks them over. She stops in front of Samson and studies him. "You are a soldier. Like me."

She moves to Yoshiko and studies her. "Are you what they call a scientist?"

"Y-yes. Do you all have the same coloring?" Yoshiko says, looking right into Captain's eyes. "Aside from the color, your eyes are almost identical to ours."

"Do you know anything about our ships?" Captain asks, not bothering to push the Doctor away.

"Not much. Mostly, it is theoretical. I have worked on some prototypes, which may have been reversed-engineered from one of your ships. You speak English." The Doctor continues to study the Captain.

Captain holds up her arm with the bracer wrapped around it. She lets Yoshiko get a good look. "My bracer is equipped with a translating device. We have a small device implanted in our ear, which receives the translation. Although your language is similar to several other planets, I have learned."

"Amazing." Yoshiko looks up and then returns her attention to the bracer. "Is it a universal translator, or does it have to be programmed?"

Yoshiko touches the bracer, but Captain pulls her arm away. Yoshiko realizes she is being impolite. "Sorry. I don't mean to be rude. The color of your skin; I was wondering..."

Captain almost rolls her eyes but shakes her head. "Commander will answer all your questions."

Captain moves in front of Brett. Yoshiko moves with her to get a better look at the bracer. Her face goes cold. When she speaks, it is in a suspicious tone. "I don't know what you are, but I don't trust you."

"I'm a mountain climber," Brett says, sounding calm.

"No, you are not." She moves closer. "I can tell you have a lot of practice at lying. I already know that the man you left behind is the climber."

"He's my backup man," Brett says with a smile.

"You are lying again. I saw the climber playing with the weapon the soldier gave him. He is not like you. Unlike you, he interests me."

Captain turns to three soldiers behind her. "Corporal, take two men and go get the mountain climber. I don't believe he is dangerous, but still, be cautious."

The three soldiers run off. Yoshiko looks concerned. She asks, "You're not going to hurt him?"

"I just said I am interested in him."

"He's harmless," Yoshiko says, smiling, returning her attention to the bracer.

"I'll let you look at it later. You are alive. Let us keep it that way."

Captain motions for them to move forward. Brett and Samson trudge off, but Yoshiko keeps pace with the Captain.

"I can't help but notice you're not wearing any breathing equipment..."

CHAPTER 23

IN NEED OF A DOCTOR

Commander sits in a small room with a long table and chairs. One of the curved walls suggests it is on the ship's rim. The walls are off-white, and small symbols decorate them. The unseen lights flicker on and off. He looks up as Captain comes in with Brett and Samson, still looking dazed. Captain looks back; this time, she rolls her eyes and goes back out. A second later, she comes back, pulling Yoshiko along.

"That wall panel, I couldn't help but notice..." she says, looking back into the hall.

Now seeming exasperated, Captain leads her to a chair by Commander and pushes along. "Commander will answer all your questions. I promise."

Brett and Samson slump into two chairs. Yoshiko sits, looking around. Two guards position themselves by the door. She looks down at the tabletop and taps it. A small holographic computer comes up. The bright blue screen is filled with what looks like gibberish. "Oh, this is interesting. There is no keyboard."

"One moment, please, scanning for appropriate language." A pleasant female voice comes out of the computer. "Is your preference Japanese or English?"

"English," she says, almost smiling. Commander watches with interest and amusement.

"Old English or..."

"Modern English is fine." Yoshiko watches the screen flick into English. She studies it. "Oh my, this is similar to Linux but more advanced."

"Pardon me, I am a little insulted. I am much superior to any of your Earth programs."

"I didn't mean to offend you. Are you an actual AI?"

"No, I am not what you would call aware. You seem to be a little more intelligent than I expected.

"Computer, you can converse later," Captain says. "Start data search for anything that will solve our present situation."

"Captain, I can do both at the same time. Oh, my apologies, you wish to converse with the Earthling. I will wait."

"This one has a lot of questions," Captain drily says.

"Let us see if we can give her some answers," Commander says, studying Yoshiko, who is still looking at the computer screen. "Check their bags."

Captain starts with Yoshiko's pack. She pulls out several things but then notices the woman pulling out her dog-eared journal. She begins to make notes. Captain comes over and looks over her shoulder. She frowns and snatches the book. "Pardon me."

"Hey, that's mine!" Yoshiko says, trying to grab it back.

Captain steps back and thumbs through it. "Commander, this looks interesting."

Captain hands the book to Commander.

"That is mine. Give it back."

"You have excellent handwriting, which will be returned to you." He thumbs through the book. It is filled with notes, sketches, and numbers. "Excellent. You know about our ships."

"No, really. Is this a typical design? Is the exterior design cosmetic, or does it serve a purpose? I didn't see any type of engine from the outside."

"Actually, you will find this interesting," the computer says. "The power source we use..."

"Later, Computer." Commander hands back her book and smiles. "You do have a lot of questions. Its design is unique. Most vessels from our world are not military. There are only twelve. We have a problem, Doctor, or is it Professor?"

"Doctor is fine. Ah, Commander, I have so many questions. I'm not sure where to start. You're not what I expected."

"You were expecting what some of your people call the *bubbleheads*? Small beings with big heads. No personality. The greys are just as bad. You are really much better off with us."

"So they are real. This is amazing. Do they come here regularly?"

"Yes; for some reason, they are fascinated with your world. I have heard rumors that you think alien visitors help build some of your past civilizations."

"Commander," the computer interjects. "I have been looking at the Earth files. That one is hilarious. If you would allow..."

"Later."

"Except for skin coloring, your appearance is so similar to ours." Yoshiko opens her journal and continues making notes. "I wonder if your internal structure is also similar."

"You have never seen our kind before?"

"My degrees are in engineering and physics with minors in Astronomy. All I ever saw were the crash sites and your ships. I assumed someone else was studying the...Oh, I am sorry."

Yoshiko stops herself when she realizes what she is saying. Commander and Captain just look at her blankly. He smiles and leans forward. "Doctor, what we have here is a misunderstanding."

Brett's face goes cold as he stares at Commander, while Samson tries to get a look at the alien weapons. Captain notes this and smiles. She pulls out her pistol and ejects what looks like a power cell. "Have a closer look. You will find it more efficient than your weapon."

"Thanks." Samson takes the pistol and really begins to study it.

Brett seems annoyed that Yoshiko and Samson are being so friendly with the alien. He sits forward and says, "A misunderstanding? You shot down two of our planes."

"First, we did not shoot down your planes," Commander says. "We collided with them when attempting to land. Our guidance system was malfunctioning. It is, as you say on Earth, a 'miracle' we were able to land. Believe it or not, we are now trapped on your planet."

Brett smiles when he realizes the situation. He leans back, looking very pleased. Yoshiko whispers to the computer, who is whispering back. Commander ignores this. "So you're stuck here. I'm in a position to negotiate."

"Surrender?" Captain snaps. "To you? To Earthlings? I don't think so."

"We don't negotiate. It is not our way. We are what you call soldiers for hire." Commander looks right at Brett. "You are not in a position to do anything."

"You're Mercenaries?" Samson says, looking up from the pistol.

"Mercenaries," Captain says. "That is a nice-sounding word."

"Captain, please. Understand this. Our ship is down, but we can more than defend ourselves. How long before your aircraft comes to drop explosive devices on us?"

Brett and Samson glance at each other. Commander smiles at their attempt not to look surprised. "Thank you, gentlemen. We now know that you plan some kind of attack. We will be forced to shoot down your planes unless the good Doctor is able to repair our ship."

"What?" Yoshiko and the computer say together.

Yoshiko looks up from the computer with a startled face. "I can't fix your ship."

"I think you can," Commander says. "You have been studying our ships. The computer can be quite helpful in this task."

"Sir, there are limits," the computer says. "The Doctor is quite bright and excellent to converse with.

Yoshiko is totally blown away and unsure of what to do. She looks at the computer. She is tempted.

"Doctor, you have spent your entire life waiting for this chance," Commander says.

"Don't try to sweet talk me. How do I know you are not the scout ship for an invading force?" she snaps.

"You see, sir," the computer says. "Her thinking is so limited. It would be like teaching the blind to see. She is an Earthling."

"Hey, I'm sitting right here." She glares at the computer. I don't know if I can trust you."

"Pardon me..." the computer says. "I have been..."

"Not you. Her."

"Oh, now I understand..."

"Computer!" Captain growls. "Who are you to judge us? Why don't you drop the little act, Doctor?"

"Little act?" She said, looking very confused. "What you are talking about?"

"Doctor, we know you haven't seen our kind before. You've had other visitors before." Commander's voice is like ice. "How many of them have you sliced up? All in the name of science."

"I would never! Besides, that is not my field."

"You have already admitted to being at UFO crash sites," Commander says.

"What do you think they do with the survivors?" Captain says. "Give them a drink and send them home?"

"I have been to the crash sites, but I never saw any survivors." She sounds defensive. "My job was to try and rebuild the ships."

Captain looks over at Brett, who seems to be ignoring the conversation. Samson watches with interest.

"Your friend didn't seem too surprised at our being here."

"Brett, is this true? Brett, have you actually seen live aliens before? Have you?"

Brett looks down.

"Brett. Tell me they're lying. Tell me we haven't done experiments on live aliens. Tell me!"

Brett just keeps looking down. Samson shakes his head, sits back, and holds out the Captain's pistol. She nods and takes it.

"Apparently, he cannot," Commander says.

"I'm not like him." Yoshiko gives Brett a cold glare. "I'm a scientist. If you promise to let us go, I'll see what I can do."

"Well, if I must," the computer says.

"You know, I know stuff you don't."

"Oh, please!"

Brett jumps up and lurches at Yoshiko. "Don't even think about helping them!"

Captain grabs him by the collar of his jacket and easily throws him against the wall, then slams the power cell into her pistol and aims it right at his face. He gives Yoshiko the evil eye. "That is all we ask. The guards will show you the way."

"Brett, we don't have the right to keep them here," Yoshiko says, getting up. She leaves with the two guards. Brett just glares at the aliens.

"We should have the mountain climber in a short time," Captain says.

"You seem interested in this man?" Commander asks.

"I'm curious. What kind of man climbs mountains for fun?"

"A crazy man. You won't be disappointed," Samson says with a smile.

CHAPTER 24

END OF COFFEE BREAK

Roscoe peeks over a rock as the aliens take away the group. He looks at the gun and back. "Yeah, that is not happening."

He sees the three aliens coming toward him and looks around.

The three soldiers come to the site. They look at the gear and camp stove. One sniffs the cup of coffee and starts to taste it.

"You're not going to drink that?" one says, looking shocked.

"It smells good. The Earthling was going to drink it," the other alien says. "I have heard these Earthlings are excellent cooks."

"I've heard that too," the last one says.

"Let them gather their stuff together and take it back to the ship," the first says.

"Don't we need the climber?" asked the one holding the coffee cup.

"You're right." The leader kneels down and tugs on the rope. "This is how they are getting down. You stand guard. We will be right back and do a sweep."

"We better check-in," one of them says. "Captain seems to want this one."

"Why? Is he dangerous?" He asks, but then taps his bracer. "Sir, the climber has probably gone back down the mountain."

"Do a quick sweep of the area to be sure," Captain says. There is a brief silence. "Wait. Did you look over the edge?"

"No sir," he says. "Hold on."

The three look over the edge but only see darkness and snow. The leader taps his bracer. "There is no one over the ledge.

"Bring in the gear. If there is a rope, cut it. Then we will sweep the area."

The leader pulls out a knife and cuts the rope. The alien, still holding the coffee cup, quickly drinks it. "This is very good."

"I told you not to drink that," the leader snaps. He grabs the cup and almost tosses it over the edge. He looks at the pot, pours himself a cup, and sips it. He smiles and nods. "This would be excellent in the morning. You stay here."

The alien watches them walk off and quickly pours another cup of coffee.

Roscoe is hanging by his hands under the overhang. He watches his rope fall by. After a few moments, Roscoe climbs back up and toward the top. He stops at the sight of the alien. He looks back down, groans, and then quickly climbs up. The alien has his back to him. Roscoe pulls the gun, looks at it, and then sneaks behind the soldier. "Hey."

The alien whirls around, and Roscoe hits him in the gut with the gun. The alien bends over. He uses the weapon to hit him on the back of the neck. He drops at Roscoe's feet. "Okay, now what. Can't climb down."

He studies the soldier on the ground. "You're kind of short."

CHAPTER 25

YOU ARE NO HELP

The engine room is circular, with two levels and a large console with multiple screens that blink on and off. There is a small metal door set into one wall. Yoshiko looks around the room with a mixture of awe and frustration. She walks around, taking a quick look at a couple of stations. Colonel is standing by the only door out. Yoshiko looks at him and asks, "What seems to be the problem?"

"Our power core is fully energized, yet we can't get our systems to function at optimum levels," Colonel says.

"So you have power, but nothing works. It's like hooking your printer to a computer. A simple fix."

"You are comparing an intergalactic ship to an Earth printer?" says the computer. "Where do I start to tell you the differences?"

"You are not helping. Use that great computer brain to think of something."

"I have no idea..."

"Shut up," Yoshiko says, looking at Colonel. "Can you explain to me how your power source works?"

"No," he says.

"I can!" the computer says.

"Do you have a liquid or dry power source?"

"I know that one too."

"I don't know," Colonel says.

"What I need is a basic schematic of your electrical system."

"What?" The computer says.

"What?" Colonel says.

"Wait, I know this," the computer says. Suddenly, a holographic image of what looks like a complex schematic appears.

"Perfect." Yoshiko moves closer to the hologram. "Show me the power source on this."

A red circle appears in the middle. Yoshiko puts her finger on it. "The power comes from here..."

"OH! OH! This is clever," the computer says. "I like this. Wait, I can highlight where we are getting power and where we are not."

"Yes, yes, that is a good idea. Do that."

One section of the holograph blinks green—a very small section. Another section blinks red. "See, this is good. The power seems to be backed up, like water in a dam."

"You are right," the computer says. "I apologize. You are so much smarter than I first thought."

"Don't worry about it. We may be able to figure this out."

"I have a good feeling about this."

Colonel glances at the two guards by the door, who seem fascinated with Yoshiko and the computer. "Do you need me anymore?"

Yoshiko isn't listening as she traces a red line on the holograph.

"No, you may leave," the computer says. "We are very busy here."

CHAPTER 26

ROSCOE TO THE RESCUE?

The tied-up Alien soldier is now stripped down to what looks like thermal underwear and struggles on the ground. Roscoe is now dressed in his black uniform. He lays his jacket over the man. "Sorry. I am pretty sure your buddies will be back before you freeze to death. I hope."

Roscoe picks up the alien's weapon and begins to fumble with it. It suddenly goes off, firing several red blasts. The laser blasts completely vaporize a rock.

"Samson would love this, but I don't want to disintegrate anyone." He looks down at the struggling alien. "I don't suppose you want to give me some pointers. Guess not. Oh, wait!"

Roscoe finds a dial on the side of the gun. It is set at the highest setting. He turns it down to the lowest setting. He picks up a small black cylinder and presses a red button on the side. It begins to beep. The beeps get louder and faster. Roscoe looks at it, and suddenly, it hits him. "Damn!"

Roscoe throws it over the mountain edge and hits the dirt. There is no explosion, just a loud *whooping* sound. He crawls over and looks over the edge. Most of the overhang is now gone. The edges of it are red hot. Sparks drift around it. "God, I wish Samson were here. Can't believe I am saying that."

Roscoe gets up, picks up the alien rifle, and walks off. "All you got to do is get us up the mountain.' Should have seen this coming."

Samson lies on one of two cots built into a small cell wall. The walls are white. The unseen light blinks on and off. Brett paces back and forth. He stops to push against the metal door.

"The door slides," Samson says, lifting his head and looking amused.

"We got to do something." Brett glares at him.

"I am open to any and all suggestions," Samson says, getting comfortable again.

"We better come up with something real quick. You really think these aliens will just let us walk out of here?"

"Us, maybe. Yoshiko? Never. They need her. What do you think Roscoe is doing?"

Roscoe slowly creeps up to a high snow drift. He stops to take in the battle disk. It is enormous, with turrets on the top. By the looks of it, the spacecraft has several levels. There are no windows. The entrance sits open with a ramp. Two guards stand by the door. Other soldiers come and go. They give each other a salute, arm across the chest. "Wow. One door and no welcome mat. You know, Roscoe, this rarely works in the movies or TV."

Roscoe watches for another minute. He sighs, pushes down the visor on his helmet, and walks right toward the ship. He reaches the ramp and gives them the salute. They return it. Then Roscoe walks right onto the ship. He comes into a curing white-walled hallway. Other aliens just walk by him. He begins to wander down the hallway. After a few minutes, he stops. The hallway just goes on and on. He leans against the wall. A door slides open. Roscoe ducks inside and pushes up his visor. He is standing in a small cabin with a bed, desk, chair, and two cabinets. Roscoe slumps onto the bed and looks around. "This ship is a maze."

"Sir, if you are lost, you may want to consult the ship diagram," the computer says.

"Looking for holding cells."

"Next level down. Section 13." A hologram appears in front of Roscoe. There are two blinking red dots and a jagged line between them. "Point A is your position. Your destination is at point B."

"Thanks." Roscoe gets up, but the door beeps and starts to open.

CHAPTER 27

PROBLEM SOLVED?

Commander and Captain walk up to a set of double doors. They open before they reach them. Yoshiko comes rushing out and looks around. "Which way?"

"Left. Left," the computer says.

She rushes down the hall. The two guards come after her. They see the officers and salute. One says, "We think she has found the problem."

They rush after Yoshiko. The computer says, "Commander, I, and with some help from the Earthling, may have found the problem."

Captain and Commander walk off in the direction of the guards.

Yoshiko comes into a small, round room with only one workstation. There are several monitors. Some are just flashing on and off. Most have green and red lines, with the red lines blinking. She looks around the room. "Where is it?"

"The black panel with the knobs. They should twist off," the computer says.

"Okay, let's do this." Yoshiko goes over to the panel and twists the knobs. "Righty tighty. Lefty loosey."

"That makes no...oh wait. Yes, it does. Very clever."

The two guards rush in and watch her. One steps forward and says, "You are supposed to stay with us."

"Yeah, yeah," Yoshiko says, getting the last knob undone. "Help me get this off."

The two men help her get the panel off and onto the floor. Inside the small compartment is a device with two golden orbs connected by a silver axle. Dozens of very thin rods are pressed against the surface of the orbs. Green lights run along the silver axle. Yoshiko looks surprised. "I don't understand."

"Neither do I," the computer says. "This is the only logical solution."

"But there it is." She looks at the device closer.

Commander and Captain come in and watch. Yoshiko moves closer. Captain steps forward. "Careful. That is the Quester Channeler. It is the heart of the ship. It gets very hot."

"Yes, the computer told me that," she says, not looking back. "Computer, this should be giving off some kind of heat."

"Yes, that was why Captain was warning you to be careful," the computer says.

"You are so sly but so am I." Yoshiko said reaches in and grabs the device. The silver needles pull back. She easily lifts the device out and holds it. "It's too light."

She puts it on the floor and studies. Commander and Captain move closer. So do the guards.

"Let me see. Let me see," the computer says. Captain pushes back one of the guards, to which the computer responds, "Thank you."

"Uh-huh!" Yoshiko said, twisting two snaps and opening the bag. Inside was nothing except a small black box. "Computer, what is this?"

"OH! OH! That is so clever and sneaky," the computer says. "It is what you would call a microprocessor. It is more complicated than that. But it is the reason my scans show the device was working."

"It's a fake," Yoshiko says, getting up. "I hope you have another one...wait. You shouldn't have been able to lift off without this in place. That would mean..."

"Someone replaced it after liftoff," Commander says.

"That would mean you have a traitor onboard. That doesn't make sense. Why would one of your own betray you?"

"Sadly, Doctor, greed is everywhere in the universe. We get the real Quester Channeler, and the ship is fixed."

"Yes, but," Yoshiko says, "According to the computer, it will take time before you can lift off. The ship was damaged during the crash. Apparently, there is a small fracture in the hull, which would be bad once in space."

"But the ship's internal repair bots should be able to repair all those things," the computer says.

"Computer, are those like what we call nanobots?" Yoshiko asks.

"Well, yes, but ours are quite superior."

"Of course they are. This was a simple fix. The computer and I figured it out in a few minutes."

"Exactly. The Doctor and I work well together. We make an excellent team. You really should convince her to come with us."

"Computer, I am right here."

"That is quite obvious."

"Commander, didn't someone check this?"

"Someone did check." Captain says in a cold tone. "Apparently, he lied."

"According to your computer, I can start rebooting everything once we get the device. Actually, the computer will be doing that."

"Exactly," the computer says. "The Doctor just has to be stationed in the engine room. When all the monitors are green, we can lift off. For some strange reason, my work has to be approved. I would take the opportunity to point out..."

"Later, Computer. When you get the part, prioritize the engines and life support systems," Commander says.

"There should be spare..." Yoshiko pauses. "What did you call this thing?"

""Questor Channeler," the computer says. "We have four."

"I have my doubts about that," Captain says.

"Stay with the doctor," Commander says to the guards. "No one comes in but Captain or myself."

Both men salute and station themselves by the door. The officers leave. Yoshiko wanders around the room. She occasionally smiles or nods at the guards.

"You should come," the computer says. "We can have fun together. This game of Chess interests me."

"You would like it, but I am not very good."

"Still, it would be fun. I would have someone to talk to. The techs are all business. You know stuff."

"Yes, I do. Tell me about your world."

CHAPTER 28

THE TRAITOR

Colonel is sitting at his desk, nervously fingering a small black box. When Commander and Captain come in, Colonel jumps out of his chair.

"Please pardon the intrusion," Commander says, stepping forward. Captain stays by the door. "The doctor has solved our problem."

"That's wonderful. When do we lift off?" He absented-mindedly wipes sweat from his brow.

"Something is bothering me," Commander says. Captain wanders over to one of the cabinets.

"Bothering you, sir?" he asks, watching Captain.

"After the crash, I first asked whether the Questor Channeler was still functioning."

"Commander, it was and probably still is. This Earth woman..."

"The Doctor, with the help of the computer, discovered the fake device. Who do you think sabotaged my ship?"

"Are you accusing me of sabotage?" He tries to sound defiant.

"According to supply, we should have three of them in stock," Captain says with a smile. Then she moves so fast that Colonel is caught completely off guard. She slams his head down onto the desk and twists his arm until he screams in agony.

"I will rip this out of its socket," she growls, "then move on to the other arm unless you tell Commander where the parts are."

"I don't know!" he screams. "I am innocent!"

"We both know I don't like you. So you can only imagine how much I am enjoying this."

"Please...I really don't..."

Captain twists his arm. There is a loud snap. She lets go of his arm and moves on to the next one. His scream is loud and pain-ridded. He begins to sob. She moves to the other arm. "No! No! In the cabinet!"

Captain, looking disappointed, let's go of the arm. She quickly opens the cabinet and throws the uniforms to the floor. Four Questor Channelers are sitting inside. "Pity. You were telling the truth. I at least got to break one arm."

"Why?" Commander asks.

Captain continues to look through Colonel's cabinet. Colonel nervously watches her, then moves behind the desk and slumps into the chair. He cradles his broken arm. "Why? I just spent a year fighting for what? The occasional reward. A handful of jewels. Do you mind...?"

"No, she doesn't. You were saying? That handful of jewels would have made you a rich man. Most of the men in my command are retiring. A well-deserved retirement."

"You would never understand. You and Captain love this life. The rules, the discipline, the fighting..."

"As an officer, you have always been a disappointment. I should not be surprised. With whom are you working?"

"My brothers should have been here by now. I don't know what is delaying them." He looks over as Captain pulls two silver canisters.

She looks at the labels and holds them up. "Salaton gas. Hook up these canisters to the life support systems. The whole crew would be dead in seconds."

Commander thinks for a moment and then sighs. "Disable the ship, use the gas to kill us, and the ship is yours. You wait for your brothers to arrive and take off with the jewels. Where were you planning on going? The rest of my command would be hunting you."

Colonel moves his unbroken arm behind his desk and looks down. Captain watches him and slowly drops her hand over her pistol. "To De-Ra 6."

"The pleasure planet. That would be the first place they would have looked. Not well thought out. Like this plan. You miscalculated and pulled the part when we were too close to Earth's gravity. We got sucked in, and here we are. How long before your brothers arrive?"

"I have no idea..." Colonel yells, grabbing a pistol from a desk drawer. The Captain pulls her pistol and shoots him. Colonel looks at the burning hole in his chest with a look of disbelief as he slumps to the floor.

"I apologize, sir. I overreacted." Captain doesn't look the least bit sorry, considering the smile on her lips.

"A whole year, and he suddenly finds his courage. Have the body cared for and get the part to the Doctor."

Captain grabs one of the devices.

Commander stops her, kneels down, and picks up the small black box. "It's a tracking device. We can expect company at any time."

"Perhaps we can change their minds." Captain takes the device and crushes it under her boot. "We can hope they are not close."

"I want to be off this planet before the late Colonel's brothers arrive."

Captain and Commander start to leave.

"Oh sir, I was distracted by working with the doctor, and now this," the computer says. "I assume you are not aware there is another Earthling onboard?"

"Another Earthling?" Commander says.

"He didn't act like a soldier. Talked to himself."

"Computer."

"This Earthling used the computer to locate the holding cells. Oddly, he climbed up through the roof panel when Colonel came in."

"The mountain climber," Captain says with a smile. "He got onto the ship. I have to meet this man."

CHAPTER 29

NO KILLING. UNDERSTAND?

With his helmet visor down, a soldier walks down the hallway toward two guards holding rifles. The passing soldier slams his rifle into the gut of one of the guards and hits the other guard in the face with its butt. He pulls off his helmet. It's Roscoe.

Samson and Brett look up when the cell door opens. Roscoe steps in and tosses a rifle to Samson. Samson smiles. Roscoe smiles back and says, "I am tired of saving your butt. I even brought you a gift."

"Thanks, I didn't get you anything." Samson checks the weapon as Roscoe pulls one of the guards into the cell.

"How about you getting me the hell off the ship, and I get us down the mountain before we both die.

Samson is examining the weapon and looks at Roscoe. "With this, no problem."

"Where's Yoshiko?"

"Good question. She's helping the aliens fix their ship," Brett growls as he pulls in the other guard and takes his weapon.

"So the ship is broken? Doesn't that change things?"

"Yes, it does," Samson says, adjusting his weapon. "We don't need to kill anyone, just stun them. Our plan is, we put on the uniforms, find the doc, and get out."

"Not to sound overly cautious, but how long before bombs start dropping?"

Brett looks at his watch. "Six hours. More than enough time to pull this off."

"Brett, we don't need to turn this into a blood bath," Samson says, standing and using his height and mass to intimate him. "Stun only."

"Got it," Brett says, showing the same settings on his weapon. "Set on stun."

CHAPTER 30

TIME IS UP

Deacon is sitting at a setup of a radio transmitter. He holds the mic close to his lips. His voice shows concern, but not his face. "Ground Hog to Snow Bird. Ground Hog to Snow Bird, come in. Groundhog to Snow Bird."

Parker studies the mountain. He turns, watches Deacon while he takes out another cigar. "Looks like your people ended up like mine."

"Yours came down alive," Deacon said, looking up. "It could be a radio malfunction. Or they have been taken prisoner. But why would they do that?"

"The storm is breaking up. I've got the go-ahead once the sky is clear," Parker says, not looking happy about it.

"That would mean your planes would be here in less than two hours."

"Sorry, Deacon, Washington agrees with me. You've lost contact with your people. We have to assume they're dead or captured."

"That's my point. Our visitors let your men go, but they took my team captive. Why...there has to be a reason. Something I am missing."

Parker takes out his lighter and lights the cigar. He looks at Deacon. "You are right, but we just don't know. I don't like it, but I've got to call in the strike. You would do the same if it were your call."

Deacon turns off the radio and closes a file on his desk. "You are right, General. We must consider the big picture."

"Sorry about your people."

CHAPTER 31

NOT SO GREAT ESCAPE

Roscoe, Samson, and Brett come out of the cell wearing black uniforms, holding helmets and rifles.

"So, which way do we go?" Samson asks.

"That way." Roscoe points down the hallway. "But I wandered around for twenty minutes looking for you guys."

"You mean you guessed we were in there?"

"No, no." Roscoe looks around. "The ship's computer was more than happy to help."

"You used the computer?"

"No, she just volunteered."

"She?" Samson asks.

"The computer sounded like a very sexy woman."

Brett is scanning the hallway. As he moves forward, a door opens, revealing a stairwell. "We got stairs here."

Roscoe walks down to a set of double doors which open automatically, revealing an elevator. Samson joins Roscoe. "I came down in this."

"So we go up," Samson says.

"That would be my guess."

Brett is looking down the stairwell when ten aliens in black uniforms come around a corner, spot the three men, and raise their weapons. Samson shoves Roscoe into the elevator, diving in after him. The doors close while Brett ducks into the stairwell.

Samson and Roscoe check their alien weapons.

"How many shots do you think these things have?" he asks.

"Good question. I know these things have a power charger of some kind," Samson says. They both look at the floor indicator. "We going up or down?"

"Like I would know," Roscoe says. "We lost Brett."

"Looks like it's just you and me. Finding the doc just became a lot harder."

"Now, is that because the aliens know we escaped, or you are teamed up with me?" Roscoe asks.

"Both."

Brett runs down the narrow stairwell, ducking yellow laser blasts. The shots hit the stairs and walls but did no damage. He comes to a door and runs out. Brett runs down the hallway as the door crashes open. The aliens chase after him.

Commander and Captain watch as Yoshiko installs the Questor Channeler. "How are we doing?" Commander asks.

"Excellent," the computer says. "Now, just let it slip down on the cradle. It should automatically hook up."

Yoshiko lets go of the device. All the silver prods reconnect the golden orbs. There was a small flash of light, followed by a hum. The hum becomes louder and steadier. A green glow fills the chamber. Monitors begin to click on. Alien symbols fill the screen. The lights stop flickering. She smiles. "I believe we are in business."

The Commander and Captain happily look at the monitors.

"Well done, Doctor!" Captain says.

"Doctor, how fast can you get the sensors up?" Commander asks.

"I thought you wanted the engines and life support," she replies.

"We found our traitor, but he has partners on the way. I don't want to be surprised."

"Let me get back to the engine room, and I'll let you know."

"Sensors are not a problem," the computer says. "I already have repair bots making repairs. The Doctor and I should have no problem from this point on."

"Thanks for the vote of confidence. You can call me Yoshiko."

"Oh, thank you, that is very kind of you."

Captain's bracer beeps; she touches it. "Report."

"The prisoners have escaped," a female voice says.

"Escaped? Explain."

"It has to be Roscoe," Yoshiko says.

"Who is Roscoe?" Commander asks.

"The mountain climber," Captain says, looking at Yoshiko. "Does he have military training?

"No idea. I just climbed with Roscoe. From that, I learned he can be very creative when needed."

"I have to meet this man," Captain says.

Then I suggest you go arrange an introduction," Commander says.

"Sir, the prisoners have weapons. They have them set to stun. I have given orders to take them alive," the voice on the bracer says.

"Yes, I want them alive." Captain salutes Commander and quickly leaves.

"I have never seen her so interested in a man before," Commander says. "Up to this point, I thought she was indifferent to men and women. Interesting."

Roscoe and Samson come out of the elevator. They look around and frown.

"This place is like a maze," Roscoe says.

"Gotta be a pattern. This is a military ship," Samson says. "There is always rhythm and reason to the layout. We just haven't figured it out."

They walk down to where four hallways meet. Roscoe looks down one of the hallways. Aliens appear at the end of both hallways. Samson pushes Roscoe down one of the empty hallways. "Run!"

"I am running!" Roscoe calls, already bolting down the hallway. The Aliens open fire. Yellow beams fly after them. Samson shoots back as he follows Roscoe. The two patrols meet at another cross-section to continue the chase.

Brett fires over his shoulder as he runs down a hallway with aliens not far behind him.

Roscoe and Samson take cover behind a stack of barrels and fire at their pursuers. Roscoe nudges Samson. "I hope there is nothing explosive in these cans!"

"Just shoot!" Samson yells, looking at him and then at the cans.

"Here's another thought. How many aliens are on this tin can?"

"Well, they just helped free a whole planet from some bad guys."

"So, a lot."

"Yeah, a lot."

More aliens come up behind and start firing. Roscoe and Samson duck down.

Samson says, "We need a plan."

"I bet you that's exactly what Custer said," Roscoe says.

"Gentlemen, is this all really necessary?" the computer asks.

Samson looks around. "Where the hell did that come from?"

"Sounds like that sexy computer I told you about," Roscoe says. "I am guessing helping us is out of the question?"

"Are you talking to me?" the computer asks. Obviously, I can't help you. Oh, thank you for the sexy remark. I am flattered. I think you should consider surrendering."

"Let us think about it," Samson says, ducking down as laser blasts fly over his head.

Brett is still being chased down the hallway. He ducks into a room. It is someone's quarters. He throws down his helmet and rubs his head. "Think. Think! Think."

"You should think about surrendering," the computer says. "You are outnumbered..."

"Who said that?" Brett yells, bringing up his weapon.

"The ship's computer. Sir, you are only prolonging the eventual outcome."

"Never!" Brett yells and runs out of the room.

"Oh, wonderful, I think that man may have some mental issues."

Roscoe and Samson are still smoking behind the barrel.

"Still thinking?" the computer asks. "What is the point of all this? I really would like to know."

Roscoe asks, "Do you have a plan?"

"Just one." Samson pulls an alien pistol from his belt. "Follow me."

"Where?"

"Just follow, and don't forget to keep shooting." Samson jumps up and blasts away with weapons. The aliens are caught by surprise. Quite a few go down. "Come on!"

Samson charges down the hallway. A shocked Roscoe watches him, jumps up, and chases after him. "This is not a plan!"

"I agree with you completely, sir," the computer says.

The aliens retreat but keep firing. Samson stops, breathing hard. "Why did they fall back?"

Roscoe runs up and stops by Samson. "You really need to work on your plans!"

"Once again, I agree with you. It's only luck that you were stunned. It is still not too late to surrender."

"I am still thinking!" Samson yells.

"Perhaps you should stop firing your weapons," the computer interjects. "It would give you time to think this out."

"The computer has a point," Brett says.

"Still thinking."

"Oh yeah, this is working out just fine."

"Sarcasm?" the computer asks.

"Yes," Roscoe says.

"Then that was quite clever."

"Will you stop talking to her?"

Brett runs up to a door and goes in. The aliens stop by the door and regroup while checking their weapons. They charge into a large room filled with boxes, barrels, and other equipment. Brett pops up and starts to fire. His laser blasts are now red. All the aliens drop to the floor with smoking holes in their chests. Brett looks like he just had the time of his life.

Roscoe and Samson are running again, returning fire when they can. An alien soldier comes out of a door. Samson knocks him to the floor and goes in. "Roscoe here!"

Roscoe follows him and stops. They find themselves in what looks like a barracks. There are aliens all over the long room. Some are lying on the cots, others are in mid-dress while others are cleaning their weapons. One small group is playing an alien card game with round cards. The door closes behind them.

"Good choice," Roscoe says and smiles. "Sorry. You all look busy. We will just leave."

The aliens start to notice the intruders. Everyone is stunned. Roscoe reaches behind them, searching for any kind of button. No one is moving.

"This is a perfect time to surrender," the computer says. "Just put your weapons down."

"Open the door," Samson says.

"Shouldn't we listen to the nice computer?" Roscoe asks.

"Open the door."

"I'm trying. Don't bother to get up."

"Please, there is no need for violence," the computer says. "Why can't you just put down your weapons?"

"Try harder."

Some of the aliens start to pick up their weapons. Roscoe is now banging on the wall while watching the aliens. "Please. We come in peace."

"It would be easier for them to believe that if you put down your weapons," the computer says.

"Open the door!" Samson yells.

The yelling snaps the aliens out of their shock. They start to grab their weapons, and several of them fire. Samson returns their fire. A few aliens go down. Yellow and red laser blasts fly at them; the red ones leave burning holes in the wall.

"Open the door! Open the door! Now!"

"Fine. I will open the door!" the computer says.

Roscoe is back up against the door. It opens, sending Roscoe to the floor. Samson dives out. They crawl out of the line of fire. The door closes. Captain and more soldiers come around the corner. Samson spots her.

"Thank goodness," the computer says. "Perhaps this can put an end to this insanity."

"Bad news. The A-team," Samson says.

Roscoe gets up and spots Captain. They both just stare at each other.

It's Kismet.

Roscoe smiles. Captain almost smiles. Samson pulls Roscoe down the hallway. The Captain's men open fire at the running men. She pushes up their weapons. "They have no place to go."

"Captain, I have tried to reason with them," the computer says. "I have a feeling the one called Roscoe wants to surrender."

"Let's give him the chance," Captain says.

"Who's the cute alien?" Roscoe asks, looking back occasionally.

"Later, Romeo. I'll introduce you if she doesn't kill us first," Samson yells.

"She is Captain," the computer says. "She seems very interested in you."

"Really?" Roscoe stops and looks back. "Well..."

"Come on," Samson yells, grabbing Roscoe and pushing him forward.

"Hey, I just want to talk to..."

"This is not date night! Now move."

They run down a hallway, with Captain and her men behind them, but at a slower pace and without firing.

"Want me to open a door?" Roscoe asks.

Samson stops at the door and opens it. They duck into the room. The Captain and her men walk up. One man starts to go in. "As you were. They are trapped."

A lot more soldiers run up, looking ready to rush in.

Samson and Roscoe come into an enormous room filled with shelves and racks of weapons. Samson looks around. "Dead end."

Roscoe looks around, slumps to the floor, and drops his weapon.

"We're trapped. Now, can I talk to the cute alien?"

"Sir, she is just outside," the computer says. "Just open the door."

Samson walks around the room, checking out the weapons like a kid in a toy store. "Well, they won't take us without a fight."

"What do you think they're planning?" Roscoe asks.

"No idea."

"Liar."

"Getting Reinforcements, securing their position, figuring out how to blast us out of here, or they could just cut off the air."

"All right, all right, I get the picture. We are screwed."

"Gentlemen, it is only logical for you to surrender."

"I agree with the computer," Roscoe says.

"I am thinking," Samson says.

"Again, with the thinking. When will your friend make up his mind?" the computer asks.

"I don't know. It must be a soldier thing."

CHAPTER 32

WAIT, WE'RE THE BAD GUYS?

Captain and her men watch the door. The Commander and Yoshiko come up.

"They are contained in the armory," Captain says. "Two of them. The soldier and mountain climber. I have teams looking for the third."

"What do you think they will do?" Commander asks.

"The soldier will try to hold his ground or fight his way out, but this mountain climber is like the Doctor says. Clever. I saw it in his face. He will try to think his way out."

"Captain, you are quite right," the computer says. "I believe he wants to surrender. It is the soldier who is still thinking. I have no idea what about it. The mountain climber is curious about you."

"Is he?" Captain asks with another almost smile.

"He thinks you're cute."

Once again, she almost smiles.

"Let me talk to them," Yoshiko says.

"Unfortunately, we cannot talk until they open the door," Captain says.

"I can," the computer offers.

"Let me go knock on it," Yoshiko says.

"Once again, I can talk to them," the computer repeats.

"Talk," Captain smiles. That's what the mountain climber will do. He'll try to talk his way out."

"How?" Commander asks.

"I don't know, but seeing what he comes up with will be interesting."

"Is anyone listening to me?" The computer says.

Samson picks up a large, nasty-looking weapon. It looks like a futuristic mini-gun with lasers, and he begins to examine it.

"Why is Yoshiko helping the bad guys?" Roscoe asks.

"Roscoe, they may not be bad guys," Samson says, looking up from the weapon.

"Come again?"

"They crashed here. They might be defending themselves until they can get their ship repaired."

"Let me get this straight. The guy we have been shooting are not invading our planet?"

"No, they are just trying to get home."

"Suddenly, I don't feel like the good guy anymore."

"Oh, this is excellent," the computer says. "We are now all talking. Things can be worked out."

"Roscoe, I just want to get out of here." Samson holds up the weapon and smiles. "I have another plan."

"Let me guess. It involves that new toy of yours."

"Look at it. This'll do some major damage."

"What happened to just stunning the aliens?" Roscoe says. "It sounds like you. Are you suggesting we blast our way out?"

"Blasting?" the computer says. "There is no need for blasting. Let's just keep talking."

"It's that or wait until they cut off the air or something else," Samson says.

Roscoe looks around the room and sigh. Samson continues to fiddle with the weapon. He spots a box of white rags and smiles. "Samson, I've got a plan. A good plan."

"Oh good, good, good. Let's all listen to what I am sure will be an excellent plan."

Five alien cooks are working in the ultra-modern galley. Brett comes in and watches them. The aliens see him and slowly raise their hands. Brett smiles and cuts them down with red laser blasts. "Sorry. No prisoners."

Captain, Commander, and Yoshiko wait outside the armory. Captain's men are positioned all over the room with their weapons ready. The door slides open. Everyone tenses. A broom handle comes out with a white rag tied to the end.

"Commander, he is not going to fight," Captain says.

"Computer! Tell them we want to talk!" Roscoe calls out from the room.

"Sir, they want to talk," the computer says.

"I heard him." Captain smiles.

"A white flag means he wants to talk," Yoshiko said.

"We are listening."

Roscoe walks out, waving the white flag. He has a weapon in his other hand. The aliens aim their guns. Captain motions them not to fire.

"Are you surrendering?" Captain asks.

"Not today, maybe tomorrow," Roscoe says.

Captain is confused and looks at Yoshiko.

"It's a joke. Earth humor," Yoshiko says.

"Earthling," says the computer, "now is not the time for Earth humor."

"Sorry," says Roscoe. "My bad."

The Captain still doesn't understand and returns her attention to Roscoe.

"How you doing, Yoshiko? I'm told you joined the other side." Roscoe keeps his eyes on Captain. She looked right back.

"It seemed to be the right thing to do," Yoshiko said. "Roscoe, we need to talk."

"White flag. Let's talk." Roscoe smiles, waving the white flag, but winks at the Captain. She is still trying to figure out how to respond.

Brett sneaks down the hall and stops when he sees the large group of aliens. He raises his weapon when he sees Yoshiko standing with aliens and Roscoe holding a white flag. "Traitors."

Yoshiko starts to move forward, but Captain stops her. "I will speak to this mountain climber."

Captain pushes her back as she moves toward Roscoe, who backs up. "Not too close, my friend says you're the best."

"I am. What do you want to talk about?"

"I think we have similar goals. I think we both just want to get the hell off this mountain."

"And your point is?"

"You need Yoshiko to fix your ship. I have no problem with that. Heck, give me a wrench, and I'll help. But once it's fixed. We all walk away."

"You are really not in a position to demand anything."

"Demand? Who is demanding? Well, my friend is a weapons expert. Right now, he has a very nasty weapon pointed at your ship's hull. Has a spinning thing on the end. It probably fires a lot of times. You can imagine what it will do."

"I don't have to. I know the weapon and its capabilities."

"You attack or cut off our air; we start putting big holes in your ship. No one goes home."

"You just walk away?" she asks. "You think this will be that easy?"

"I have found very few things are easy."

"I could say yes now and no later."

"You could, but you're a soldier like my friend. I suspect, like him, you have a code of honor."

Roscoe puts down his weapon and steps back. Captain smiles, puts away her pistol, and makes a hand motion. The troops put down their weapons.

"So you climb mountains for fun."

"Yes, I do."

"Why?"

"Why not?"

Yoshiko walks up and smiles at Roscoe. Commander just watches them. Samson comes out and watches the alien soldiers leave. "Thanks for telling me the war is over."

"War is over," Roscoe says, not looking at Samson. He is completely focused on Captain. She is just as focused.

Samson puts down the weapon. Commander and Yoshiko leave. Samson notices the Captain and Roscoe haven't moved. "I better go with the Doc."

Samson walks off. Roscoe and the Captain are alone.

"Please tell me, why do you climb mountains for fun?" Captain asks.

"Why are you a soldier?" he asks.

"It is what I am good at and enjoy."

"That's why I climb mountains."

"I'm not sure I understand."

"It is hard to explain to someone who has never climbed a mountain. It's like you are testing yourself. When I am hanging on the side of a mountain, I feel really alive."

"I think I understand."

"You don't have mountains on your planet?"

"Of course, big ones like this. Many of your centuries ago may have been climbed, but there is no record. If we want to go to the top, we use our airships..."

"Excuse me, you have mountains on your planet that no one has ever climbed?"

The Captain's bracer beeps. She glances at it. "I must go."

"Oh, Captain, I left one of your guys tied up by my gear."

"I know. We found the soldier. He will be disciplined. Your ropes and such are here on the ship."

Captain walks off. Roscoe watches her walk away. She turns and looks at him. "What are you looking at?"

"You got a great walk."

"Thank you." Captain is obviously confused, shakes her head, and leaves. Roscoe looks around and realizes he is alone. "Hey, where is everyone? I need some help. Computer? Computer? I know you can hear me. Which way?"

Laughter fills the hallways.

"Oh great, I got a computer that's a joker."

CHAPTER 33

BRETT'S GONE BYE-BYE

Brett moves down a hallway, spots stunned alien lying on the floor. He takes the alien's helmet and puts it on. A small group of aliens runs by. He joins them.

Yoshiko is still working on one of the consoles in the engine room. A lot more of the equipment and monitors seem to be working. Captain comes in with guards carrying Roscoe's climbing gear. They put it on the floor.

"I thought the mountain climber would be here?" Captain asks.

"His name is Roscoe. I think he is lost on your ship. The Commander went to find him."

The computer snickers. Yoshiko looks at it. Captain comes over. "Computer, have you found the other Earthling?"

"I was monitoring him, but he put on a helmet with the visor down. He moved into a group of your troops and I lost him."

"Find him. We have dead bodies."

Samson, Roscoe, and Commander come into the room. Roscoe goes to his equipment and checks it. Samson looks around the room while Commander joins Yoshiko at the console. The soldiers start to walk to the door. Another soldier comes in, raises his weapons, and shoots the soldiers. Brett pushes up the visor on his helmet. Roscoe jumps up and moves toward Brett. "Brett, relax, we made a deal!"

Captain and Samson make moves for their weapons. Brett fires red blasts over their heads. "Nobody move! Lose the hardware! Now!"

Captain, Commander, and Samson drop their weapons. Brett kicks them and looks across the room.

"Brett!" Roscoe says, moving in front of him. "Put down the gun. Everything is cool. They're going to let us go."

"You believe that!?"

"Brett, there are no bad guys here. It's just a bunch of guys trying to get home. So why don't you just put the gun down."

Brett fires over Roscoe's head, making him jump back.

"Okay, you keep the gun. Can I ask what you think you're doing?"

"My job. Which is more than I can say for you traitors," Brett says in a very frantic voice, his face sweating. The weapon trembles in his hand. He looks over the engine room. "So this is the engine room."

"Brett, what are you doing?" Yoshiko asks. "Do you have a plan?"

Brett nervously moves around the room, taking it all in. He points his weapon at Captain. "You! Captain, lock the door!"

The Captain just stands. Roscoe watches Brett point the weapon at her.

"Do it now!" he screams.

"Okay, Brett has gone bye-bye," Roscoe says.

"Shut up Roscoe!" Brett snarls. "I am sick of your little remarks."

Captain doesn't move. Brett steps closer. Roscoe moves in front her. "Back off Brett."

"Sir, I have secured the room," the computer says. "There is no reason to harm anyone else."

"Okay, what next?" Roscoe asks.

"We have Commander and Captain, and we are holding the engine room," Brett says with a very scary look. "We control the ship."

"There are a few guys outside that might try to change that," Roscoe says as he unzips his jacket.

"Commander is going to order his men to lay down their weapons."

"Never. Especially to someone like you," Commander says in a calm voice.

"Then I'll have to kill you." Brett moves closer with the weapon up.

"I am not afraid of death." He looks straight into Brett's face.

"Sir, you don't understand the culture and code Commander lives by," the computer says. "These actions will only result in your death."

"SHUT UP!" Brett screams, aims the weapon at Commander, and fires one shot, hitting him in the shoulder.

"Give the order!"

"I would rather die," Commander says, putting his hand on his shoulder. Brett aims at the man's chest.

"Brett, killing him gets you nothing." Roscoe still stands in front of Captain. "Think about what you're doing. You are dealing with aliens. They don't think like you."

"He is right," Computer says. "If you kill Commander and Captain, I will have no choice but to open the door. I have alerted the crew of the situation. There are quite a few of the crew outside. You will die for nothing."

"I could kill the doctor," Brett says, aiming the weapon. "With her dead, you are stuck here."

"The major problem has been solved," Computer says. "I can finish all repairs on my own. I should also inform you. I have been monitoring your people's communications. They have moved up the time of the attack."

"What? They can't."

"A fog bank has moved in, temporarily delaying their takeoff. I estimate they will arrive here in less than two of your Earth hours."

"Deacon," Brett snarls and begins to pace around the room. He stops at looks at Yoshiko. "The doctor is going to radio Deacon. He will call off the bombers. He'll have an army up here in minutes."

"The radio is history. You checked it yourself," Yoshiko says.

"That's right. I disabled it," Brett says more to himself than anyone else. "Bad move on my part. Wait, this is a space ship. It has to have a radio."

"This is a ship from another planet," Yoshiko says. "No pun intended, but their equipment is alien to me."

"Suddenly you don't know anything. It looks to me like you just don't want to help me, Doc."

Yoshiko starts to look over the console, but it is obvious she is stalling. Roscoe slowly lifts the back of his jacket. The pistol that Samson gave him is stuck in the middle of his back. Captain smiles and slowly raises her hand.

Samson is wrapping a cloth around the Commander's shoulder. Roscoe catches his eye and nods. Brett leans against the wall, letting off a deep sigh, holding his weapon on them. "I'm still waiting, Doc."

"I am trying my best," Yoshiko says. "The computer refuses to help. Besides, she will probably block the signal."

"Is that right?" Brett yells looking around the room.

"Yes, sir," the computer says. "My priority is to protect the ship. I really don't see how you will escape."

"This is a flying saucer." Brett moves even closer to Yoshiko. "We have a chance to take it intact. Think of what we'll learn. It'll be all yours to study."

"What about the crew?" she asks.

"We can learn a lot from them too," he says with too big a grin.

"I'm learning a lot right now."

"What's that supposed to mean?" Brett snarls. "I am handing you the chance of a lifetime. All you have to do is make a simple radio call."

"She's saying you are one screwed up psycho!" Samson snaps

Brett straightens up and points his weapon at Samson. Captain grabs the pistol. Roscoe drops to the floor, giving Captain a clear shot. "Do it!"

Captain fires three shots. The bullets hit Brett in the shoulder and arm. Samson sweeps out his leg and knocks Brett's feet out from under him. Samson is up and slams his fist into Brett's face.

"Well done," the computer says.

"If this weapon hadn't jumped, I would have killed him," Captain says, looking at the pistol. "I suppose with practice you can adjust for that. Still, not a very practical weapon."

The doors open. Soldiers and aliens dressed in jumpsuits rush in. The medics kneel down by the commander.

"Deacon told me to keep an eye on Brett." Samson says. "He suspected he might be losing it," Samson says, looking down at Brett. "I had no idea he was just plain crazy."

"You knew this and didn't share?" Roscoe asks.

"That sounds like something we should have known," Yoshiko says.

"I agree," the computer says. "We could have avoided this whole situation."

"Fine." Samson raises his hands in defeat. "My bad. His last mission was a simple break-in. Get the data and leave. By the time he was done, the building was in flames and twelve men were dead, including his partner."

"Nice to know our government is still using only the best," Roscoe mumbles.

"Sarcasm again?" the computer asks.

"Yes."

"Oh, I am learning so much about Earthlings today."

Captain watches the medic and soldiers secure the engine room. "Take care of Commander and that man. Security, stay with the prisoner. He is dangerous."

The med team begins to work on the wounded while security stands over Brett.

"I think the best course of action would be to throw him off the ship," the computer says. "Problem solved."

"I agree." Captain looks over the pistol. "I would like to practice more with this."

"Keep it," Roscoe says. "A gift."

"Thank you," she says. Samson starts to say something but then changes his mind.

"Doctor, can we lift off?" Commander asks, ignoring the medic working on his shoulder.

"Computer," Yoshiko asks, "how long?"

"Give us an hour," the computer says. "Maybe less."

"Captain, prepare the ship for liftoff." Commander says as he is helped to his feet.

"Yes sir." Captain exits the room, and Roscoe goes after her. Yoshiko smiles as she returns to her console.

"Interesting," says the computer, "what is happening between the one called Roscoe and Captain. I am curious to see how it ends."

"You and me both," Yoshiko says. "Okay, let's get the scanners up. We want to spot those planes before they spot us."

CHAPTER 34

OPPORTUNITY KNOCKS

Captain walks down the hallway still studying the pistol. Roscoe runs up and stops her. She looks pleased but still doesn't smile.

"Captain," he says, almost touching her but stops himself.

"Yes, Roscoe is your name?" she asks.

"You know my name. What's your name?"

"Captain."

"Well, that is a mouthful. Ah, maybe I should just call you Captain."

"It might be best. To be honest, I never cared for the name my parents gave me."

"Okay, look." Roscoe tries to collect his thoughts.

She looks a little confused. "You wish to say something?" Once again, the smile is almost there.

"On our planet, we have a saying. Opportunity only knocks once."

"What is *opportunity*, and why does it only knock once?" she asks, looking more confused.

"Opportunity. Good luck? Chance?"

"I know what chance is."

"This like a chance meeting. You try to make the most of it, because you may never see that person again," Roscoe says.

They turn as two of the med team bring out Brett with the security team on their heels. Yoshiko emerges with the two meds and the wounded Commander.

"Doctor, please return to your station. I will be fine. Go," Commander says. Yoshiko watches the Commander leave with the meds. Roscoe and the Captain move down the hall. Yoshiko smiles and ducks in the doorway.

"I could be wrong," Roscoe continues. "Really wrong but I think there is a connection between us. I can just feel it."

"I think I understand. I must be honest with you. I am not good at expressing myself when it comes to this kind of situation. Most males and females I have met have been disappointing."

"Ah, ah, I don't know what to do here. I mean..."

"I have seen many of your Earth films. So maybe this will help." Captain pulls Roscoe close and gives him a long, passionate kiss. Both really enjoy it. She pulls away and finally smiles. "On my planet, we have a saying. The white bird flies in the sky when you least expect it."

She gives him another quick kiss and walks off.

"The white bird? I wasn't talking about birds. When did birds come into the conversation?"

Yoshiko walks up and grins. "Roscoe, let me give you a hint. The white bird is love." She turns and starts to walk away. "I think it's a beautiful metaphor."

Roscoe is left alone in the hallway. He begins to walk and then stops. "Oh, geeez, not again."

He looks around and slumps against the wall. Then looks up at the ceiling. "Don't suppose you are going to help?"

The computer laughs. "Oh sir, I am learning so much."

CHAPTER 35

UNEXPECTED VISITORS

A Triangular shaped ship comes around the moon. It is a good sized ship, with a dull green hull marked with scorch marks, dents, and other damage. It may have been a beautiful ship at one time but is now just old and ugly.

Two Gargonians stand in a small room that serves as the bridge. The walls may have been once white, but now it is hard to tell what color they were. There are holes in the walls and floor, with silver cables poking out and snaking along the floor to the three consoles manned by two more Gargonians. The room is dimly lit by greenish lights.

The Gargonians are tall, slender beings with sickly yellow skin. Their eyes seem too big for their faces while the nose is nothing more than a bump. Two thick lips and yellowish teeth add to their ugliness. They are wearing red and black jumpsuits that have seen better days. Ripped and dirty, their clothes hang on their slender frames.

"We have lost the signal," one of the aliens says.

"The downed ship could be anywhere," the other says. "I don't want to waste time looking for it. This Earth, is there anything of value here?"

One of the technicians looks up from his console. "Their technology is quite primitive. The inhabitants would be good for slaves. They do have minerals that would be of value."

"We have no time to dig," the lead Gargonian says. "We need a place to land and grab as many slaves as possible. Young would be better."

"I have found several stockpiles of what the Earthlings call *gold*," the tech says. "It is what we call *krain*."

"How much?"

"More than enough. One place is called Fort Knox."

"Sounds like a military base. Move on."

"A city called Moscow. Wait. I found a high concentration buried under a building called United States Federal Reserve. We can blast through the building and surface, then use our mago-beam to pull it up. There are a quite a few of the Earthlings in the city. We could get some slaves along with the krain."

"Good. Put us in orbit. Ready the crew."

"Will the others interfere?" one alien asks.

"According to the ones we tortured, the ship is helpless. The crew might even be dead. I didn't come this far to go home emptyhanded."

CHAPTER 36

Captain is working with a four man crew on an octagon-shaped bridge. All the stations are working. Commander, his arm in a sling, comes onto the bridge.

"Commander on the bridge!" One of the crew yells.

Everyone snaps to attention. Captain is pleased to see him. He smiles and sits in his command chair. "As you were. Status report."

"All sensors and life support are online."

Captain nods, looking around the room.

"We should be able to lift off in twenty minutes."

"Excellent." Commander hits a button on the arm of his chair. "Doctor, well done."

"All readings seem to be normal, but keep in mind I am trusting the computer." Yoshiko's voice fills the room.

"Everything is fine," Computer says. "You don't trust me?"

"Okay, I trust you. I am just nervous."

"As you Earthlings say, I got this."

"Understood," Commander says with a smile. "You had better start packing. And, Doctor, no souvenirs."

"I guess I'll have to unpack some things. Tell Roscoe and Samson I'll meet them by the engine room."

"I will arrange for security to escort the one called Brett off the ship."

"Delay that until the last possible moment," Commander says. "He is still dangerous."

Captain nods and returns to her duties. Roscoe and Samson come onto the bridge and look around.

"Looks like you are up and running," Samson says, taking it all in.

"This so cool," Roscoe says, wandering around. One of the crew looks at him with confusion.

"We will be lifting off shortly, so you must keep your farewells brief," Commander says.

Roscoe and the Captain stare at each other. Finally she looks away and pretends to fiddle with a control panel. Roscoe walks over and touches her hand. She turns to him. "Listen Captain…"

Suddenly an alarm sounds. Red lights blink on and off. The crew starts to work their stations while the Captain hits a button and watches a monitor fill with alien symbols.

"Excuse me," Captain says, looking at the screen. "Switching to deep scan with multiple terms. Locking on."

"Identify."

"Readings coming in. Standard power readings. The power readings are coming back a little unstable. Triangular shape. No markings. Completing scan. I have positive I.D. It is an old Tritan battle cruiser. Not in very good condition. It is manned by Gargonians."

"Gargonians?" Commander asks. "They are a little far from home. What would be here that they would want?"

"Who or what are Gargonians?" Roscoe asks.

"The Gargonians are raiders. They usually roam their own systems preying on primitive planets like yours, but I have never seen them in this sector."

"So we are a primitive planet?" Samson asks.

"Yours weapons cannot match their weapons. They could cause massive damage and take countless lives. Then they would plunder anything of value, including taking many of your people to be sold as slaves. They never come out this far. Why?"

"Did you say something about the traitor having brothers? This could be them," Roscoe says.

"No." Captain looks up. "This is not them. They trust no one but their own. But, if the brothers were caught by the Gargonians, they would have talked."

"The Gargonians could have learned about our cargo," Commander says.

"What cargo?" Roscoe asks.

"Our payment from out last employers," Commander says. "We have what could be considered a great fortune of sparkling gems onboard."

"They will attempt to disable our ship before we can lift off," Captain says. "Their ship is no match for us in space, so their only chance is to take us on the ground."

"It will take time to get a weapons lock, but in the meantime let us get you off my ship," Commander says.

The Captain looks at Roscoe. It's obvious they want to talk. The Commander motions for her to follow him. Roscoe and Samson follow them off the bridge.

CHAPTER 37

ROSCOE, YOU'RE THE BEST

Yoshiko is standing in the middle of the engine room watching all the monitors. Some of the screens show percentage bars slowly rising. "Okay, okay, we are almost there."

"Yes, we are," the computer says. "Yoshiko, you really should stay. There is so much to see out there. Think of the fun we will have."

She is about to answer when Commander, Captain, Roscoe, and Samson come in. "Is there a problem?"

"Some bad guys just showed up. We got to go now."

"Oh, Gargonians," the computer says. "I don't see the problem. The Gargonians are not targeting us."

Commander goes to the console and hits a button. "Bridge, what are they targeting?"

"They appear to be targeting a city called New York," a man's voice says.

"So they are here to rape and pillage our planet? Which means they don't know about you," Roscoe says. "That's good."

"Or they don't know where we are," Commander says.

"I smashed the tracker," Captain agrees. "They came looking for us and are now settling on whatever they can steal from Earth."

"This is not good. So what do we do?"

Commander looks at Yoshiko and asks, "Doctor, can you give me the turbo lasers and defense grids?"

"Commander, what are you intending do?" Yoshiko asks. "We almost have the ship ready for launch."

"If you can give me my weapons, I'll give them another target."

"Weapons are coming up," Yoshiko says. "The defense grid will take longer. They are not completely powered up."

"Sir, we will have some defense grids but not at full power," the computer says. "My scans show it will take time for them to find us, even with scanners. They have not maintained their ship very well."

"But if he fires," Yoshiko says, "they will know exactly where we are."

"Commander, that is crazy," Roscoe says. "That ship is going to blast you off this mountain."

"It our fault they are here," Captain says. "We have seen what they do to worlds like yours. We cannot allow that to happen. We couldn't live with ourselves."

"Commander, I appreciate what you're trying to do, but getting yourself killed won't help," Samson says. "After they kill you, they will still be here."

"Bridge, lock turbo lasers on the Gargonian ship and fire on my command," Commander says. "I can't return to my world leaving that scum here."

"Locked on," a voice says.

"As a fellow soldier," Commander continues, turning to Samson, "you should understand. Fire."

One of the turrets on top of the disk spins, points up, and fires off three purple laser blasts.

The three shots hit the ship, doing no real damage, but it veers away from the Earth.

Commander turns to Roscoe, Samson, and Yoshiko. He just shrugs as Captain watches a monitor.

"They now know we are here," Commander says, casually.

"Commander, they are no longer targeting New York," Captain says. "They're moving into position to target us."

"Doc, any chance you can get the ship off the ground before they start shooting?" Samson asks.

"Impossible," Yoshiko says. "I can give you part of the defense grid, but I don't how long it will last."

"Too bad we just can't teleport up to their ship and take it out, like in that T.V. show," Roscoe says.

"Teleport?" Captain asks.

"It was a TV show had a machine that would take you apart and send you to another place."

"Modular Transfer. We have such a device. We don't use it often for obvious reasons."

"You're kidding, that is so cool."

"It's not cold at all. Why would it be cold?"

"No sweetie, cool..."

"Later. So we can get men over to that ship. Do some damage?" Samson asks.

"The problem is, we only get four soldiers over before they block our signal," Commander says.

"Four guys can do a lot of damage...especially if they plant a bomb."

"An excellent plan. I think. What is a bomb?" Captain asks.

"It's an explosive device," Samson says.

"We have no major explosives on board."

"How much explosives do you think crazy old Brett brought with him?" Roscoe asks.

Samson smiles. "Let's find out."

Suddenly, the whole ship is shaken by something hitting it. They all look up.

"They are trying to get a lock on us," Captain says.

"As I stated before, they have not maintained their ship. The core is unstable," the computer says. "If this explosive is powerful enough, we can plant a bomb by the power core and destroy their ship."

"Computer, that would not be possible," Captain says.

"How hard can it be?" Samson asks. "We plant the bomb and leave. I have done it too many times to count."

Captain goes to a small metal door built into the wall and opens it. "See for yourself. It would have to be placed at the bottom, next to the core."

Samson and Roscoe come over and look in. There is a wide, circular open space with pipes, wires, and cables running up and down the wall. It five levels high. At the bottom what looks like a glass dome. It is filled with swirling colors. It gives off a humming sound.

Samson turns away from the door and looks at Captain. Roscoe continues to look over the chamber.

"Maybe we could drop it?" Samson suggests.

"The bomb must be right next to the dome shield to be effective," Computer says.

"It is impossible to reach," Captain explains. "Techs use hovering packs to make repairs. I have a feeling the traitor disabled them or just left them. It is impossible."

Roscoe turns to the group and smiles. "Impossible? I don't think so. Guys that is an easy climb. There are plenty of holds. We got everything we need over there..."

The group looks at Roscoe.

"On the other hand, it would be so dangerous. I am not sure I would have the skills..."

"Why are you lying?" Captain asks. "You climbed this mountain."

"Babe..."

"What is Babe? And you called me sweetie a while ago? Are you saying you're afraid?" Captain says, looking shocked.

"No, no..." Roscoe says.

"That's right, buddy. You're the best. You can climb anything." Samson says with a huge smile.

"I am not afraid," Roscoe says with a weak smile. "I make jokes when I get nervous. You guys are willing to risk your lives to save my planet. I am willing to do the same. Teleporting, planting a bomb in some kind of power core. It's all good."

"I don't understand your humor, but I can see you are not a coward."

"Oh, Captain!" Computer says. "*Babe* and *sweetie* are terms of endearment. Apparently the Earthling really likes you."

"Thank you," Roscoe says, looking embarrassed.

"Buddy, I'll be there to back you up," Samson says, slapping Roscoe on the back.

"Hey, don't call me buddy like we're old pals. I am just going to plant your bomb and try not to get killed."

"People, we have a plan." Samson walks over to the packs. He pulls out several blocks of explosives. "Geez, what the hell was Brett planning on blowing up? We are so in business."

Commander goes over to Samson and watches him assemble the bomb.

Captain moves closer to Roscoe. "I will be there too...sweetie."

"Thanks, babe." He almost kisses her but stops when she gives him a cold look. "Right, wrong. Wrong time."

They go over to the packs. Roscoe starts to check his equipment. Captain kneels down and watches both men with interest.

"I can't see what he is doing," Computer says.

Commander steps back a little.

"Thank you."

CHAPTER 38

PUTTING OUT THE TRASH

Brett is lying on a bed in the cell. His unzipped jacket shows he has bandages around his arm and chest. The whole cell shakes. He looks up when the door opens. The guards are gone. Brett rolls out of bed and peeks out the door, pulling a knife out from his boot. The hallway is lit by flashing red lights. Smiling, he makes his way down the hallway.

After a few twists and turns, he comes to a stairwell door. Brett climbs to the next floor. He peeks out the door. The hallway is empty. He creeps out. After few minutes, he comes to closed door. There is a control panel by the door. Brett moves to it and almost pushes a button. Instead, he looks at the knife, nods, and start to go down the hallway. A heavy door slams down, stopping him.

"Oh no you don't," the computer says. "Not again."

"Who is that?"

"Using a phrase I don't completely understand: I am your worst nightmare," the computer says. A door behind Brett closes. A hissing sound starts.

Brett grabs his ears and yells, "What are you doing?"

"Creating a small vacuum. Don't worry it won't kill you...well, it would in time, but I won't let get that far."

"Stoppppp!" Brett screams, grabbing the sides of his head.

The main door opens. Brett is sucked out of the ship and lands in a pile of snow. The door closes. He quickly zips up his jacket and begins to shiver.

"I suggest you move away from the ship," the computer says. "We are about to take off, and that will result in your death."

"Computer?" Yoshiko asks. "I got a red blip by the main hatch?"

"It should go away. I suspect someone was just putting out the trash," Computer says.

"Oh, back to green. We're good."

CHAPTER 39

IT WILL BE SO EASY...

Samson is adjusting the timer attached to blocks of explosive, packed into a backpack. He looks at up at Roscoe, who adjusting his harness. He slings a coil of rope around his chest.

"This is what we call a suicide switch," Samson explains, pointing to the device. "Once you press it, nothing in the world can stop the bomb from going off. It's not like TV where you can cut the wire at the last minute."

"Nice to know, since I am the one going down and pushing the button," Roscoe says, not looking thrilled. "How much time do I have?"

"How much do you need?"

"Five minutes down. Ten minutes up. Make it fifteen. No, twenty."

"You push the button at the bottom. I'll give you fifteen."

"I need twenty."

The ship is hit, another blast shaking the whole thing. Roscoe and Samson look around.

"You can do it in fifteen; you're the best. Besides, we may not have twenty minutes." Samson looks back at Captain and Corporal - a short female with short hair. They are both dressed in black combat suits holding weapons. Captain hands Samson a rifle and vest with hand grenades on it.

"We can't wait any longer," Captain says. "This is Corporal, an excellent soldier. I have fought with her many times."

"What's the layout of this ship?" Samson says. "I don't want Roscoe getting lost again."

"I doubt they will have a computer with warped sense of humor," Roscoe says.

"I have scanned their system," Computer says. "It is quite archaic. I have managed to shut it down in the engine room. The Gargonains will not know you are there until it is too late."

"We should appear right inside the engine room," Captain says. "There should be minimal resistance."

Roscoe watches everyone check their weapons. "Where's my weapon?"

"You need your hands for climbing," Captain says. "I will cover you. Samson and Corporal will watch the door."

"A pistol?" Roscoe asks. "A small pistol?"

"Very well, if you insist," Captain says, reaching behind her back and pulling out a small silver pistol. "This is small, so it won't be bothersome for you."

Roscoe takes the weapon, which just fills in the palm of his hand. He looks at Captain. "Kind of small."

"I just told you that. It is an excellent weapon."

"Good things come in little packages," Roscoe says, pushing the pistol into the middle of his back.

"Now you are joking again, but no one is laughing. I don't understand. It might not be time for jokes."

"You got that right, Captain," Samson says.

The Corporal looks at Roscoe and the rope. "So you are going climb down into the core, plant the device, and climb back up. That is insanity. It cannot be done."

"You have never seen me climb," Roscoe says. "This will be so easy."

CHAPTER 40

IT IS NEVER EASY...

The small room has two blue daises in the center. An alien soldier stands behind a console. He is making adjustments. The dais begin to give off a blue glow. A low humming fills the room. Roscoe walks up to the daises.

"No, this doesn't look dangerous at all," says Roscoe.

"It is very dangerous," Captain says. "It is why we only use this device as a last resort."

"Who goes first?" Roscoe asks.

"I will go first to secure the area," Captain says.

"I'm going with you," Samson says.

"As you wish." Captain looks at Roscoe. "I...I would not be pleased if you came to any harm. Be careful...sweetie."

"Babe, with you watching my back," Roscoe says, "Nothing is going to happen."

"Thank you." She nods and then gives him a quick kiss. Captain and Samson climb on the dais. She hits her wrist communicator. "Standing by."

"We have another problem." Commander's voice fills the room. "Our scanners are picking up some planes moving in our direction. I estimate thirty minutes to arrival. I assume the bombs will start dropping soon after that. I advise you to be quick."

"I thought you could take them out?" Samson asks.

"Do you really want us to shoot down your planes?" Commander says.

"Good point. We better move," Samson concedes.

Captain nods at the man at the console. "We are ready."

The blue glow becomes brighter and brighter. Then, suddenly, they are gone

"I've changed my mind," Roscoe says.

"Please joke later," Corporal says, pushing toward the daises. He climbs on and sighs.

"Beam me up Scotty," Roscoe says.

"What?" Corporal asks as the blue glow engulfs them.

This control room is smaller and dirtier, with fewer work stations. Two of the monitors are broken. Several large pipes crisscross the room. Captain and Samson appear behind a large pipe in the corner.

"That was interesting," Samson says.

Captain doesn't say a word. She peeks around the pipe. Four Gargonians in red and black jumpsuits are fiddling with the controls. She steps out, shoots them while showing nothing. She walks over and checks the bodies. Samson runs to the open double doors and peeks out.

"We are clear out here," Samson says.

"Be ready," Captain says. "The computer may be shut down, but there are many eyes on this ship."

Captain goes to the metal door and opens it. This power core is smaller, and much dirtier. There are cables dangling down. There are occasional sparks flying into the air. The core at the bottom glows red. She turns back when Roscoe and Corporal appear in the room.

"I didn't like that," Roscoe says.

"No one does," Corporal says, joining Samson by the door.

"The technicians are taken care of," Captain says. "We must still move quickly."

"Maybe we can plant the bomb and get out before they know we were here," Roscoe says.

"If opportunity is with us," she says with a smile, "and it knocks."

Roscoe goes to the hatch, looks inside, and smiles. "Piece a cake."

"Now is not the time to be thinking of food."

"I meant it was going to be easy." Roscoe pulls off the rope, wrapping it around a pipe.

"What does cake have to do with climbing?" she asks.

"Let me explain..."

"Roscoe! We don't have time for this!" Samson yells. "Just plant the bomb."

"I'll try to explain later." Roscoe gives Captain a quick kiss. "A last kiss before I die."

"You will not die. I won't allow it. Now climb."

"You heard the Captain: move your butt!" Samson says.

Roscoe clips the rope to his harness and climbs out into the core. He quickly takes in his surroundings before looking down. He begins to rappel down, making it look so easy. Captain watches with great interest. She turns to Samson and Corporal, watching the door. Captain says, "This is amazing. Corporal, you should see this. He makes it look so easy."

Corporal starts to go over but is stopped by Samson. He smiles and says, "I'll make him climb for you later."

Corporal returns her attention to the door. Captain looks through the hatch. Roscoe is really moving. He passes another hatch just as it opens. Roscoe finds himself suddenly face to face with a Gargonian. Roscoe swings away from the hatch as the alien aims and fires. Captain shoots from above.

The Gargonian ship shoots red lasers down at the Earth's surface.

The blasts hit around the ship, causing rocks and snow to fall onto the Battle Disk. Brett, who has been trying to get back into ship, has to duck. He runs away from the ship. The turbo lasers fire back. Commander sits in his chair, watching the monitor. The bridge crew work their stations. The ground shakes while the lights flicker

"That was too close," Commander says, looking amused.

"Sir, our defense grid is weakening," said an alien manning one of the consoles.

"Doctor, I know this is a bad time, but I need you to put up our defense grid at full power," Commander says.

Yoshiko looks at the console and monitors. Three of the monitors are flashing. "Defense grid, defense grid..."

"Second station," the computer says. "Commander, we are working on it. We should have it up in a few seconds."

Yoshiko moves to another console and begins to fiddle with the controls. "I hope you are right about this."

Roscoe is swinging around the core and fumbling for his pistol. Captain manages to kill the alien. Other hatches open. More Gargonians peek out and then lean out with their weapons. Captain keeps firing at the Gargonains. This forces them to fire down at her. Roscoe pushes out from the wall and drops.

"NO!" Captain yells.

Samson and corporal have pushed barrels into the doorway. They watch the hallway. Several armed Gargonians come charging up the hallway. Samson and the Private open fire, catching the attacker by surprise. Several drop to the floor. More aliens come and return fire.

"They figured out we are here," Samson says.

"They have discovered Roscoe!" called Captain. "I think he may be in trouble."

Roscoe slides down and stops just above the dome. He pulls off the pack, then turns so he is upside down. Laser blasts land around him and the glowing core. Roscoe opens the pack, pushes the button, and drops the pack. "Mission complete; now to get out of here."

He gets upright and starts to climb.

Deacon, Parker, and soldiers watch the laser blasts going back and forth. There are a few small explosions on top of the mountain.

"Do you have any idea what is going on?" Parker asks, holding an unlit cigar.

"No idea." Deacon watches with great interest. He pulls out a pipe and lights it. "This, as Sherlock Holmes would say, is a *three pipe problem.*"

"No argument there," Parker says and lights his cigar.

Once again, the ship is rocked by laser blasts. Sparks fly into the air around the room. The Commander looks around and hits a button.

"We have taken no major damage," the computer says. "Engines are at full power. We can lift off."

"Start liftoff procedures."

Roscoe is using the pipes to climb - and for cover. Laser blasts hit all around him. The Captain is still shooting, killing three. Roscoe pulls his pistol and starts to fire at closeby aliens. This makes them duck back inside. He frantically climbs back up but drops his pistol. He looks down. His eyes lock on the bomb, which makes him climb faster.

The doorway and barrels are riddled with smoking holes. There is a pile of bodies in the hallway. Captain looks back and yells, "He has planted the bomb! We have succeeded in saving the ship. Signal for you two to be taken back to the ship."

"No, that is not happening," Samson says. "How is Roscoe doing?"

Roscoe is pinned down between two large pipes. Laser blasts land all around him. He looks down at the bomb. "Well, now what?"

Commander looks around his bridge. Some monitors are broken. Two wounded aliens lie on the ground.

"Commander, the Gargonian ship is trying to use its targeting beams," Computer says.

"Jam targeting beams. Stand by to lift off on my order."

"Consider it done," Computer says.

Roscoe is climbing like a madman. A laser hits a pipe, making it swing out. It nails Roscoe right in the gut. The pipe and Roscoe swing out, leaving him dangling in the middle of the core.

The battle disc starts to give off a low humming, which becomes louder. A green light starts to spin around the middle of the ship.

Roscoe is still hanging. He shakes his head and swings back toward the wall. Roscoe climbs until he reaches the hatch. A laser hits him in the shoulder, making him fall a few feet before he grabs onto a pipe. Blood is running down his arm.

"Roscoe!" Captain yells.

"Ouch!" Roscoe growls as he holds on with one hand. A grunt of pain comes out as he starts to climb, wounded arm and all.

Captain watches. She looks around, throws down her rifle, and climbs out into the core. She looks terrified but gets a good grip on the rope and reaches down with one hand. "Roscoe!"

"Look at you!" Roscoe laughs as he climbs up. He reaches up with his good hand. Captain pulls him up with surprising ease. He nods for her to go in. She climbs out. Roscoe follows her. They collapse to the floor.

"You do that for fun?" she asks, looking at Roscoe. "You are quite insane."

"You're not typically being shot at while you climb," Roscoe says.

"That is a good point...sweetie."

"Let's get off this thing."

Samson and Corporal are holding their own. The Gargonians are still coming. Suddenly, a large ceiling air vent explodes. Three aliens drop down. Captain fires while still on the floor, cutting down the aliens. She gets up and takes up a position by a pipe. She shoots the attackers as they keep trying to come through.

Roscoe crawls over, grabbing a weapon from one of the dead aliens, and helps her take out the intruders. "Still got one good arm. Can we leave now?"

Yoshiko is rushing around the engine room. "Where are the repair bots you promised?"

"I didn't make such a promise," Computer says. Everything lights up.

Both Yoshiko and the Computer laugh.

"Commander, we up and running! Lift off!"

Commander smiles and hits his chair as everything comes online. Medics are helping the wounded while new soldiers take over their positions.

"Let's show them what this ship can really do."

"Commander!" the computer says. "The team is calling. Our transfer signal is being blocked."

"Not for long. Lift off!"

Squadrons of F-17s are flying toward the mountain. "Blackjack to Ground hog. Two minutes to target."

Roscoe, Samson, Captain, and Corporal are still blasting away, but it looks like a losing battle.

"We may need a white flag soon," Roscoe says.

"I doubt waving a white piece of cloth will work this time," Captain replies.

Suddenly, a blue glow engulfs Captain and Corporal. They shimmer and vanish. They both move farther back into the engine room.

"Looks like you and me again," Roscoe says.

"Not my first choice," Samson replies. "Corporal was kind of cute."

"Bad timing," Roscoe says with a small smile as more of the Gargonians charge into the room. "Least they get to go home."

"Yeah."

Captain and Corporal appear in one of the daises. She jumps down and yells at the soldier at the console. "Transfer complete. Get them back here!"

Roscoe and Samson are now backed up into a corner. A crowd of aliens is charging them. Their weapons stop firing and begin to beep.

"Can't say I am surprised," Roscoe says, looking at his weapon.

"The whole day wasn't that bad," Samson says.

They are both engulfed in a blue glow, vanishing as the Gargonians are almost on top of them.

The two men appear in the room and both fall off their dais. Captain runs up and hugs Roscoe. "Babe, are you fine?"

"Sweetie, I really hate doing that," Roscoe says.

"Excellent. You are making jokes. You will be fine."

The planes dive down at the battle disc.

"Locked on target. What the hell is that thing?"

"Cut the chatter and destroy whatever it is."

Commander watches the fighter. "Let's try to scare those planes off. Minimum charge. Quick short blasts."

One the turrets fires off several white laser blasts into the sky. The laser blast goes right through the squadron of jets, doing no damage but making them spin out of control.

"What the hell was that?"

"Break off! Break off and regroup for another pass!"

The Gargonian ship fires down at the Earth. The battle disk begins to lift off. The laser blasts come down but explode before even coming close to the ship.

The battle disk flies straight up into the sky with all four turrets blasting away. The Gargonian ship starts to take some damage, but then explodes. The battle disk moves out into space, leaving Earth behind.

CHAPTER 41

HARD CHOICES

Captain and Commander walk into in a very comfortable-looking room. The walls and carpet are a very light purple with black symbols. There is a plush sofa and chairs of a deeper purple. The tables are made of some black glass material. A long bar made of reddish wood takes up one wall. Roscoe, Samson, and Yoshiko are slumped into chairs looking at each other. Roscoe is wearing a red shirt with black pants. Samson is back in his fatigues. Yoshiko is wearing a long comfortable white robe.

"We will hide behind your moon for a day or two, then we will be able return you to Earth," Commander says.

"Commander, we been thinking. Why should we go back? But we need little more time," Roscoe says.

"I see," Commander says. "Well, you are more than welcome. Our planet is quite beautiful with its very big mountains. And you will be able to visit other planets and see things you never imagined."

Commander walks over to what looks like a window made of black glass. He taps the glass. The planet Earth appears in all its beauty. "You will be leaving your home and will never be able to come back. So I suggest you think long and hard about this. Take your time. We are in no hurry. You can use this to focus on any part of your planet, if you desire a closer look. Just tap the screen until it zooms in on the place you wish to see."

Commander walks to the door. Captain goes to Roscoe and takes his hand. "Captain! As you were. This is his choice."

They leave the Earthlings alone. Roscoe moves closer to the monitor. Yoshiko moves beside him.

"What are you thinking?" Yoshiko asks.

"Ribs," Roscoe says.

"Pardon me?"

Roscoe taps the screen several times.

"You did say ribs?" she asks again.

The screen zooms in and in, until a small wood building come into view. There is an old sign with the words, BUCKY'S RIBS.

"Bucky's Ribs," Roscoe says. "I go there at least twice a year. He makes the best ribs. Meat just falls off the bone. And the sauce? To die for. You get a stack of ribs and a couple of cold beers, find a back booth, and put some good rock and roll on the juke box."

"Good rock and roll?" Yoshiko asks.

"Really? Buddy Holly, Stones, Birds, Jefferson Airplane, maybe some CCR. You down a couple beers to get up the nerve to go over to the girl you've being watching all night and ask her to dance. When she says yes, you know you are really alive."

"I know that place. You're right about the ribs," Samson says, joining them.

"Right now I'm thinking I would love to take Captain there and slow dance with her. See her taste ribs for the first time. But that can't happen. She could never be a part of my world."

"But you could be part of hers," Yoshiko says.

"Romantic. But, the hard fact is, I have nothing back on Earth. I am a legend but too lazy to hustle. The idea of helping people get to the top of Mount Everest, risking their lives for what? A photo op? That is just too depressing to consider. There is no big money in what I do."

Yoshiko adjusts the monitor. Stan is running across campus looking very worried. She smiles and wipes away a tear. "Stan the man. Looks like he's late again."

"That your boyfriend?" Samson asks.

"No. Just a friend. We work together. I am thinking I really don't have that many friends. First college, and then my research. No time for...a life. Now that makes me sad."

"Putting UFOs back together. How did you get into that?"

"After I got my P.H.D. Deacon showed up and asked if I would like to do something really interesting with my life."

"Putting flying saucers back together probably sounded pretty exciting."

"It did at the time. But to be honest, I spend most of my days in a big windowless room with guards. Always wondering where they came from. Who built them? Almost everything it was a prototype. It was like they were testing me. You know how frustrating it is to walk around every day after doing that? Then looking up at the stars?"

"I don't have your soul. I guess it would been like me looking at a mountain and not being able to climb it."

"Yeah...Deacon always promised to get me on one of the shuttle missions."

"The shuttle would be kind of a dull ride after this," Samson says. He focuses the screen on what looks like nothing but desert. Then a few small houses come into focus.

"Is that home?" Roscoe asks.

"Such as it is. As a kid, all I could think about was getting out. You can imagine how hard it is to get off the res. That's why I joined the service. I really wanted to see the world. All I've seen so far are jungles, swamps, deserts, and the top of this mountain."

"Well, you got a chance to really see something now, big guy."

"It's more than that. I've done some stuff I'm not proud of. If I go with these guys, it would be like starting all over. Fresh and new. Clean. Maybe I could find something else to do. I know I don't have that option back on Earth."

Yoshiko taps the screen and Earth reappears. They watch it in silence.

"I wonder if they have holidays up there," she muses. "Thanksgiving was always big at my house. Everyone would go to my ma's house, she'd serve the turkey, and we would just eat and talk. Eat some more. Talk. Eat. Then we would have dessert. I think I was happiest then."

"Won't your family miss you?" Roscoe asked.

"Mom and dad passed away two years ago. My sister died last year. It is probably why I buried myself in work."

"My parents are gone, too," Samson says. "Haven't seen my brothers in years. They probably think I am dead."

"So we're all in the same boat. No family," Roscoe says. "Of course, there is Deacon to consider."

"Deacon will lock us up in one of his secret little places so he can poke and prod us," Samson says. "Then, in the interest of national security, he'll have us put away."

"Put away? Like in killing us?" Yoshiko looks shocked.

"Most likely a well-placed bullet."

"Don't sugar coat it for us Samson," Roscoe says.

"Guys, I have got to go. It's my only chance to see what is out there. I can't go back to that windowless room."

"Captain has stolen my heart. I can't live without that."

"Yeah, like I'm going to go back and facing Deacon alone," Samson says.

Roscoe goes over to a bar, opens a red bottle, and pours three drinks. Yoshiko and Samson come over. He hands out the glasses to his friends. "A toast to the planet Earth. It ain't perfect, but it was home."

"To Earth," Yoshiko and Samson say together.

They gulp down their drinks and slam the glasses on the bar. Roscoe looks at the bottle. "I wish I knew what this was. This sweet. I am going to have another."

"Excellent!" the computer says. "Oh, this is going to be so much fun."

"I am not talking to you," Roscoe says, pouring himself a drink. The other two hold out their glasses.

"You can't take a joke?"

"I suppose getting drunk would be rude or something," Roscoe says as Captain comes in and runs to him.

She hugs him and kisses him. "You're staying!"

"Really. You told her?"

"What?" the computer says.

Captain looks at the bottle. "Pour me a drink. I am off duty."

"This trip just go so much better."

CHAPTER 42

NOT A TOTAL LOSS

A helicopter comes in for a landing. A squad of soldiers jumps out and scatters. Deacon and Parker climb out and walk up to the huge black indentation in the ground. They look at it and then look up at the sky.

"How unfortunate," Deacon says. "It would have been a nice addition to our collection."

"I would think you have enough specimens for your collection."

Deacon ignores the remark and kneels down by the charred ground. He frowns and pushes away some snow. He picks up one of the alien pistols. "Ah, not a total loss. This will interest you too."

"Yeah," Parker says, getting a closer look. "Looks like it has several settings, if this can actually just stun a soldier."

"It could change how we fight wars," Deacon says. He thinks for a moment. "I'll handle the cover story."

Two soldiers drag a half frozen Brett up to Deacon and Parker. He straightens up but continues to shiver. "I have to report: the rest of the team betrayed us."

"Us," Deacon says with a smile. "You can't imagine how happy I am to see you."

Deacon opens Brett's jacket, studies Brett's bandages. He lifts the edge of one. There is a wound, but it's already healing. "Oh my, this is interesting. I think Brett should be taken back for a full examination. Of course, we will work together on this. It is too big for my small agency."

"Put this man on a chopper and get him back to base. Top security. Have the med teams study his bandages," Parker says with real authority.

"Wait! Wait!" Brett screams as he is dragged off.

"You think the rest are dead?" Parker asks, pulling out a cigar.

"I would hope they've gone somewhere that we mere mortals can only dream of."

Deacon's phone rings. "Yes, really. Excellent. I will get you clearance at once."

Deacon hangs up and smiles. "It seems there are the remains of a space vessel drifting quite close to the space station."

"So not a total loss." The general returns his gaze to the stars. "Lucky bastards."

CHAPTER 43

COMPATIBLE?

Roscoe comes through a door into a large room with a big bed, desk, small sofa, and coffee table. There is a window (or monitor?) showing an incredible view of the universe. He's only wearing a towel, still wet from his shower.

Captain is lying on the bed, wearing a green camisole and nothing else. She smiles at Roscoe.

"How do I rate such a nice room?" he asks.

"You don't. I do," Captain says.

"Oh, so these are your quarters," Roscoe says, moving toward the bed.

"Our quarters." She sits up and smiles.

"I just had a thought; we are from different planets."

"You figured that out? All by yourself?" she says with a grin.

"Well, yeah... Hey, you do have a sense of humor."

"I and the computer are learning." She moves to the end of the bed.

"All joking aside, I'm wondering if we are...uh, compatible."

"Compatible?"

"You know. Biologically."

"I just discussed that with the computer." She says and yanks off his towel. "Come here, I'll show you how compatible we are."

"What? No playful banter?"

"Come here!" She laughs and pulls him onto the bed with her. She ends up on top.

"God, you are so bossy."

"Will you shut up and kiss me!"